Books by Shirleen Davies

Historical Western Romance Series
MacLarens of Fire Mountain

Tougher than the Rest, Book One
Faster than the Rest, Book Two
Harder than the Rest, Book Three
Stronger than the Rest, Book Four
Deadlier than the Rest, Book Five
Wilder than the Rest, Book Six

Redemption Mountain

Redemption's Edge, Book One
Wildfire Creek, Book Two
Sunrise Ridge, Book Three
Dixie Moon, Book Four
Survivor Pass, Book Five
Promise Trail, Book Six
Deep River, Book Seven
Courage Canyon, Book Eight
Forsaken Falls, Book Nine
Solit
Rogu
Ang
Restle
Storm

D1265334

Mystery Mesa, Book Fifteen
Thunder Valley, Book Sixteen, Coming Next in the Series!

MacLarens of Boundary Mountain

Colin's Quest, Book One,
Brodie's Gamble, Book Two
Quinn's Honor, Book Three
Sam's Legacy, Book Four
Heather's Choice, Book Five
Nate's Destiny, Book Six
Blaine's Wager, Book Seven
Fletcher's Pride, Book Eight
Bay's Desire, Book Nine
Cam's Hope, Book Ten

Romantic Suspense

Eternal Brethren, Military Romantic Suspense

Steadfast, Book One
Shattered, Book Two
Haunted, Book Three
Untamed, Book Four
Devoted, Book Five
Faithful, Book Six
Exposed, Book Seven,
Undaunted, Book Eight, Coming Next in the Series!

Peregrine Bay, Romantic Suspense

Reclaiming Love, Book One
Our Kind of Love, Book Two
Edge of Love, Coming Next in the Series!

Contemporary Romance Series

MacLarens of Fire Mountain

Second Summer, Book One
Hard Landing, Book Two
One More Day, Book Three
All Your Nights, Book Four
Always Love You, Book Five
Hearts Don't Lie, Book Six
No Getting Over You, Book Seven
'Til the Sun Comes Up, Book Eight
Foolish Heart, Book Nine

Burnt River

Thorn's Journey
Del's Choice
Boone's Surrender

The best way to stay in touch is to subscribe to my newsletter. Go to www.shirleendavies.com and subscribe in the box at the top of the right column that asks for your email. You'll be notified of new books before they are released, have chances to win great prizes, and receive other subscriber-only specials.

Mystery Mesa

Redemption Mountain Historical Western Romance Series

SHIRLEEN DAVIES

Book Fifteen in the Redemption Mountain

Historical Western Romance Series

Avalanche Ranch Press, LLC
PO Box 12618
Prescott, AZ 86304

Mystery Mesa is a work of fiction. Names, characters, places, and incidents are either products of the author's imagination or used fictitiously. Any resemblance to actual events, locales, or persons, living or dead, is wholly coincidental.

Book design and conversions by Joseph Murray at 3rdplanetpublishing.com

Cover design by Jaycee DeLorenzo at Sweet 'N Spicy Designs

ISBN: 978-1-947680-22-7

I care about quality, so if you find an error, please contact me via email at shirleen@shirleendavies.com

Description

A dedicated lawman and single father with a haunted past.
Can he risk his heart on a young woman he'll never deserve?

Mystery Mesa, Book Fifteen, Redemption Mountain Historical Western Romance Series

Hezekiah Boudreaux's life is a sequence of surprises. The deputy sheriff in Splendor is still adjusting to the latest twist—being a single father. Hex's precocious daughter, Lucy, is a handful, and one of two females who bring joy to a life filled with ne'er-do-wells, cons, and rustlers.

Christina McKenna is still reeling from the sudden death of her twin. She fills each day taking care of her younger sister while acting as cook and caretaker for Hex Boudreaux and his always active daughter. The problem is, she's falling in love with her boss.

Both believe they have lots of time to determine their futures until the arrival of a beautiful woman in town, a murder during a birthday celebration, and a series of disastrous events force Hex and Chrissy to take a hard look at their lives.

Unraveling who to trust, who to hunt, the good from the bad, takes time—a commodity in short supply. Hex knows the longer it takes to identify the killers, the higher the danger to his daughter and the woman he's come to love.

Mystery Mesa, book fifteen in the Redemption Mountain historical western romance series, is a full-length novel with an HEA and no cliffhanger.

Visit my website for a list of characters for each series.
http://www.shirleendavies.com/character-list.html

Mystery Mesa

Prologue

Christina McKenna brushed tears from her face, staring into the open grave holding her father's coffin. Behind her, the Missouri River still roared its power, although the flood waters had receded since taking the lives of Edward McKenna and his second wife, Mirna.

Within inches of his grave was her mother's. Jillian McKenna had died young, within years of giving birth to Christina and her twin sister, Millicent. Her father had mourned the loss of his beloved wife, vowing to always love her, even as he planned to marry a woman of eighteen.

Where Jillian was beautiful, vibrant, with a big heart and forgiving nature, Mirna was immature, her cold heart holding little love for anything except their father's money and herself. The twins had taken satisfaction at locating her grave twenty yards away. Far enough from their father and mother so few would associate her with the McKenna clan. Christina and Millicent had their reasons, and both believed their father would understand.

Mirna had barely spared an hour each day with the daughter born within months of her wedding to

Edward. His older daughters had tolerated Mirna, but loved their younger sister.

Cecilia was a precious child, tagging along with Christina and Millicent even with eleven years separating them. The three made a game of hiding from their father and Mirna, keeping to themselves, preferring to eat meals early, separate from their elders.

Christina turned away from the grave, leaving the bittersweet memories behind to join Millicent and Cecilia. They stood by their coach, preparing for the ride home and another few hours of well-wishers sharing memories and food. The day couldn't end soon enough for the three McKenna sisters.

"Ladies." Their father's long-time attorney approached, fingering the brim of his black bowler, his gaze moving over them. "Again, my condolences at your loss."

"Thank you." Christina found herself struggling to remember the man's name.

Reaching into a pocket, he pulled out an envelope, handing it to her. "Your father's will. It's simple and quite clear. You and Millicent should read it and let me know a time we can meet. There are some documents you need to sign."

Taking the envelope, her chest squeezed. Each change solidified the fact their father truly was gone. "I'll send a messenger with a time to meet."

Assisting the girls into the carriage, the attorney stepped away. "Good day to you. I'll look forward to seeing you again soon." Tipping his hat, he turned, leaving their driver to take them home.

Waiting until they drove through the cemetery gate, Christina slid the envelope from her reticule, turning it over and over.

"Go ahead and open it." Millicent's curiosity spurned Christina on.

Opening it, she pulled out the documents, unfolding them so she and her sister could both read. As the attorney had said, it was clear and simple.

"Father left everything to us, Millie. Mirna and Cici aren't even mentioned." Christina's stunned expression met her twin's. "We're to be Cici's guardians, but all the assets will be transferred to you and me."

"It's quite odd, don't you think? Most husbands leave everything to their spouse? Upon their death, the money goes to their descendants or..." Millicent shrugged, looking at the document again. "You're right, though. Neither Mirna nor Cici are even listed."

Folding the documents, Christina slipped them inside the envelope, still wondering at their father's decision not to include his second wife.

"Unless a husband is quite unhappy with the woman he married." Christina leaned toward Millicent, lowering her voice so Cecilia couldn't hear. "Do you think Father regretted marrying Mirna?"

"I don't know."

They sat back, thoughts of their father's puzzling actions haunting both on the ride back to their house. They'd never have answers to so many questions.

As the driver stopped in front of their home, Millicent made no move to get out. Instead, she placed a hand on Christina's arm.

"I don't want to stay in Kansas City. I don't want to live in this house."

Her twin understood without asking. After their mother's death, everything good inside the house had vanished, replaced by a cold, stony existence. No more love or laughter. Nothing that made a house a home.

"I agree. Where would you like to go, Millie?"

Surprise flashed across her face, shocked her sister had so quickly agreed. "West."

Christina lifted a brow, one corner of her mouth tipping upward. "West?"

A gleam brightened Millicent's eyes. "We've been to New York, seen almost all the eastern seaboard. I'd like to travel through the frontier, travel by stagecoach, and see the Pacific Ocean. Think of all the wonderful places we'll see, the people we'll meet. Why, we might even see the savages Father spoke about. Wouldn't it be wonderful?"

It didn't sound so wonderful to Christina, but she refused to dampen the only happy thoughts they'd shared all day. If a change, even of this magnitude, would heal their hearts, she was all for it.

"A trip out west sounds perfect to me, Millie. Absolutely perfect."

Chapter One

Christina stood over the grave of her twin sister, Millicent, swatting tears from her face, mind going back to the day they'd sat in their carriage, planning to leave Kansas City. They'd been so excited, talking well into the night after solemn services for their father and stepmother. Both wanted a fresh start far away.

She and her sister had mapped out their journey, including taking the stagecoach north out of Denver. It was then the lives of the three sisters changed.

Millicent had taken ill within days of boarding the stage to the Montana Territory. Over the miles, she'd grown weak, until Christina made the decision to disembark in Big Pine to seek medical advice. The examination had been inconclusive, and disheartening.

The doctor had provided laudanum for pain, apologizing for not having a better diagnosis. Christina had understood his meaning. There was nothing that could be done. Prepare for the worst.

Still, she'd prayed for her twin, begged God not to take her after losing their mother and father. He hadn't responded.

Millicent had collapsed a year ago at the celebration of their friends' wedding. One moment, she stood next to Christina. The next, she'd crumbled to the floor of the church. Gone within seconds, leaving her devastated twin and younger sister alone.

"Would you like company?" The deep, rough voice came from her friend and employer, Hex Boudreaux, one of several deputies in Splendor.

She startled when he placed a hand on the small of her back, the warmth seeping through her clothes in the chilled morning air. "It would be nice, but I'm not the best person to be around right now."

Ignoring her comment, he stared at the headstone, feeling his own sorrow at the loss of a lovely young woman. "Millie was a beautiful person. Inside and out. You were lucky to have her as a sister."

"Yes, she was." She choked on the words, embarrassed at her lack of decorum.

Placing an arm around her shoulders, Hex drew her against his side. "It's not a crime to grieve someone you loved. Grieving helps you heal the pain, makes it a little easier to go on."

She'd tensed when first feeling his arm around her, relaxing at his words. "You speak as if you've had experience."

"Zeke and I lost our parents years ago. It wasn't easy. I still think about them, but it gets easier as time passes."

"They would've loved Lucy." Christina mentioned Hex's young daughter. At five, she was cute, precocious, and a real challenge.

Tightening his grip before dropping his arm, Hex nodded. "Yes, they would've."

"Did you know Millie's birthday is this Saturday?"

Chuckling, he nodded. "Millie's *and* yours. To celebrate, Zeke and I would like to take you to supper."

Surprised warmth rolled through her at the thoughtful invitation. "That's quite nice of you. What of the girls?"

He feigned a shiver, making Christina smile. "I wouldn't dare celebrate your birthday without them. What do you say?"

"It sounds wonderful. Thank you."

Taking her arm, he hooked it through his. "If you're done here, I'll walk you back to the boardinghouse. Luce and Cici will be out of school in a few hours."

Hex referred to her job of watching the girls between their discharge from school and when he returned home after his shift. Some days, Hex invited them to stay for supper. Most times, she'd take Cici with her to the boardinghouse, they'd share supper, read, then go to bed, starting the routine again the following day. It had become tiresome months ago, but she refused to quit.

Christina and Cici didn't need the money. Their father had left enough of an estate so they could live in comfort the rest of their lives. What she did need was the chance to see and talk with Hex each day.

She knew he saw her as a girl, not a young woman of twenty. A woman who'd fallen in love with him. It was a fact she never planned to voice.

They waved at several people they knew as they traversed the muddy street, doing their best to avoid the remaining patches of snow. Christina hoped there'd be ingredients to make snacks for the girls when they arrived after school. If not, she'd be making a quick trip to the general store.

Splendor had grown significantly since Christina and Cici arrived, numbering over eight thousand residents. Additional veins of gold had been found at the Devil Dancer mine, requiring doubling the number of men. The local bank manager, Horace Clausen, told Hex he'd been contacted by investors in the Midwest inquiring about opening businesses in Splendor. The number of ranchers had doubled, most buying property east and south of town.

In addition, the Pelletier ranch, Redemption's Edge, continued to expand, as did Dominic Lucero's spread. Both had begun crossbreeding short and longhorn cattle. Their efforts were starting to payoff.

Hex stopped in front of the house he shared with Lucy and Zeke. "I'm going to get to the jail, Chrissy. The door's unlocked, and there are supplies to fix the girls something after school. I also bought milk from Suzanne."

He spoke fondly of Suzanne Barnett, one of the owners of the town's boardinghouse and restaurant. It had been built long before most locals had heard of Splendor.

"Do you need anything else?" As had become his habit, Hex studied her face, looking for signs of fatigue. Millie's illness had taken a lot from her. Coupled with taking care of Cici, the emotional and physical toll had been great.

"I'm fine, Hex. You worry too much about me." She wished the worry had come from love, but knew it was his natural tendency to protect others. His job as a deputy fit him well.

Reaching out, he touched the tip of her nose with his forefinger. "I suppose so." A brief smile appeared before he turned away.

Christina stepped onto the small porch of the two bedroom home, watching him disappear around the corner of the school teacher's house on his way to the jail. He'd be gone until almost sunset, giving her plenty of time to prepare food for the girls and clean the house.

Hex and Zeke never asked her to pick up after them, make beds, or sweep the floors. She found the work kept her busy, allowing her time to think about the future.

Christina knew there'd be a day when Hex would fall in love and marry. He needed a wife and mother for Lucy. There were several women who'd be interested in a life with the rugged lawman, including the school teacher, Sarah Murton.

She thought of Millicent and her dream of seeing San Francisco. Christina had heard Caroline Davis had spent a year in the city overlooking the Pacific Ocean. Isabella Dixon had gone with her, both returning to Splendor to marry the men they loved.

Grabbing a broom and dustpan, she got busy with cleaning while considering inviting both women to have lunch with her. She had so many questions about the rapidly growing city, as well as the journey from Splendor.

Christina didn't plan to leave soon. Cici loved living in the frontier town, the friendships she'd made, and acting as a big sister to Lucy. She'd coped well with Millie's death, reminding Christina her twin was in a place without pain, where everyone loved her.

The words of nine-year-old Cici often soothed her when missing Millie. As twins, they'd had a special relationship, at times sharing thoughts without speaking.

Tossing clothes onto the beds in the room shared by Hex and Zeke, she continued sweeping, again thinking of the changes in Splendor. During the last year, newcomers had opened a meat market and bakery, tailor shop, Apothecary, and small bookstore.

Allie Coulter had told her she planned to expand her millinery and dress shop to include the sale of dry goods. The general store carried several bolts of fabric, but not the selection required for a large population of women who sewed clothes for their entire family. Christina had no doubt more stores would be opened.

Moving to the kitchen, she whipped up a batch of gingerbread cakes. Knowing both Hex and Zeke had a sweet tooth, she checked the cupboard, pulling out ingredients for spice cake. When spring came, she'd be able to get lemons to make a lemon pie, one of Hex's favorites.

She smiled at the thought of him. He always made her feel welcome, appreciated her help around the house and with Lucy. Christina had begun to consider renting one of the empty houses on the street. There was one next door, but she discarded it as being too close to Hex. She definitely didn't want to know when he courted another woman, which would happen at some point.

On another street, next door to Travis and Isabella Dixon, was another empty house. It had two bedrooms with a large living room and decent kitchen. She'd already spoken to Noah Brandt about it, as he'd built most the houses in town on land owned by his wife, Abby. If all went as planned, Christina and Cici would be able to move in within the month.

She jumped at the front door slamming open, laughter accompanying the girls as they ran to the kitchen. "Ladies, what have I told you about slamming doors?"

"Don't do it," Lucy answered.

Cici tried without success to hide a grin. "Sorry, Chrissy. We came to get you."

Crossing her arms, she lifted a brow. "Why's that?"

"You have to see the wagons driving through town. They're filled with girls and boys." Cici followed the wonderful aroma to the wood stove. "What are you baking?"

"Gingerbread cakes. In fact, they should be ready." Removing them from the oven, she shooed the girls away. "You need to let them cool for a few minutes."

Lucy's lower lip protruded. "But we'll miss the wagons."

Removing her apron, Christina hung it on a hook. "While they cool, you can show me the wagons. Not for long, though. I have to get supper started."

The girls shrieked, Lucy grabbing her hand. "We have to hurry, Chrissy. Even Hex is outside watching them."

Christina allowed the girls to tug her along on their way toward the jail, where'd they'd seen Hex. The boardwalk was crowded with onlookers watching two covered and two open farm wagons roll through town. Additional horses were tied behind each wagon. She suspected they'd stop by Noah's livery, a common spot for newcomers.

Instead, the lead wagon pulled to a stop in front of the jail, the driver jumping down to approach Hex. Holding out his hand, his gripped Hex's.

"Sheriff, I'm Finn Hanrahan."

"It's *Deputy* Boudreaux, Mr. Hanrahan."

"Call me Finn." He swept an arm toward the street. "As you can see, I've got four wagons full of family. We plan to make Splendor our home. Let me introduce you."

Stopping at his covered wagon, he yelled for his wife and daughters to show themselves. "Deputy Boudreaux, this is my wife, Dara, and my daughters, Alana and Brenda."

Hex's gaze landed on the two stunning women, his mouth going dry as he focused on Alana. Shining red hair and green eyes which sparkled with mirth. Swallowing the growing lump in his throat, he removed his hat.

"Ladies. Welcome to Splendor." Hearing the huskiness in his voice, Hex cleared his throat. He couldn't remember the last time a woman affected him as immediately as Alana.

"We are so glad to finally get here, Deputy," Brenda answered, looking up and down the boardwalk.

Alana's cheeks flushed at the interest she saw in the man's eyes. "Deputy."

"The next wagon is my brother and his two sons. The third and fourth are my cousins and their children. You'll be meeting them at some point." Finn laughed, sending Hex a knowing grin. "Don't want to overwhelm you."

Hex didn't care much about who was in the other wagons. All his attention remained focused on Alana. "Where will you and your family be staying?"

"We bought a few acres of land south of town. We'll be building four houses while we open our businesses."

The comments had Hex switching his gaze to Finn. "What businesses are you in, Mr. Hanrahan?"

"The saloon business, Deputy. We've already ordered what we need, and plan to open within a few weeks."

Hex nodded, wondering if Nick Barnett knew of their plans. He and his partners owned the Dixie and Wild Rose saloons. Both had eliminated their upstairs business, renting the rooms to travelers instead of offering them for pleasure.

The third establishment, Ruby's Grand Palace, was owned by Ruby Walsh and offered a variety of entertainment. Music, dancing, and anything else a lonely cowboy might want.

"Is that right?"

"It is. I've already rented the building. As I recall, it's next to the newspaper. I expect it will be the best saloon in Splendor. Alana, Brenda, and their cousins will be serving and providing entertainment."

Hex's eyes narrowed on Finn before shifting to Alana. "Entertainment?"

"No, no. Nothing like what you'd be thinking. They sing and dance. You'll have to come watch the show."

Hex definitely would stop in to watch. "I just might do that, Finn."

"Well, we should be going. It'll be dark soon and we want to set up camp on our new property. Good day to you, Deputy."

He touched the brim of his hat. "Finn. Ladies." Standing back, he watched the wagons continue their journey, a slight grin curving his lips. Yes, he definitely would be one of their first customers.

Chapter Two

Christina stood unnoticed on the boardwalk. She'd overheard it all, her stomach clenching. *Alana.* It was a pretty name for a beautiful young woman. Of course Hex would find her attractive. Any man would.

"Aren't they interesting, Chrissy?" Cici held her hand, watching the wagons drive out of town.

"Yes, sweetheart, they are. We should get back to the house so I can get supper going."

"Will we be staying to eat with them tonight?"

Christina hesitated a moment. After what she'd witnessed, it no longer appealed to her. "Not tonight. Suzanne is expecting us at the boardinghouse. She's fixing roast and berry pie tonight. They're your favorites."

Without another word, and before Hex could see them, she whirled around, walking swiftly back to his house. She had a little less than three hours to get supper ready and prepare dessert so they could leave the instant Hex got home.

Christina thought of the house she planned to rent next door to Isabella. After what she'd heard and seen, she felt much better about her decision not to rent a place close to Hex.

It was for the best. She knew the day would come when Hex met someone who caught his attention. A stunning Irish lass with glorious red hair and flashing green eyes.

"What can we do, Chrissy?" Cici looked up at her, always ready to help cook. Lucy stood beside her, never showing the same enthusiasm about lending a hand.

"How about you two bring in some more firewood for the stove? Afterward, you can help with the potatoes and carrots."

She stood at the sink, watching as they rushed from the house. Both loved to play outside. Christina doubted they'd return before twenty minutes had passed. Taking the few steps to the stove, she stoked the fire. There was plenty of firewood to get through supper and breakfast the following day, but chores would keep the girls busy.

She made the vinegar pie, sliding it into the oven, then returned to the counter. The already cleaned chicken lay in the sink. With practiced hands, she cut it into pieces, slipping the pieces into the simmering pot of water on the stove before pulling potatoes and an onion from a burlap sack. She'd start peeling, more for something to do than because of lack of time. The girls could take over if they returned before Christina finished. If not, there were still carrots to prepare.

Lost in the work, she stared out the window above the sink to the vacant house next door. It wouldn't be long before someone would move in, maybe one of the new deputies the sheriff planned to hire.

She liked the way so many new people were stopping in Splendor, deciding this would be the place they'd start a business, raise a family. Before the girls were released from school, she'd often spend time in the new bookstore next to the meat market and bakery.

Although the space was small, it was stocked with dime novels, and books on science, nature, and antiquities. She limited herself to buying one book every two weeks. When she and Cici moved into one of Noah's houses, she'd build shelves to hold her purchases. At night, under the glow of a fire, she'd read...and dream.

The back door being kicked open bit into her thoughts, turning her attention to the young girls with sticks of firewood in their arms. Without direction, they added them to the stack by the stove, brushing hands down their dresses.

"Wash your hands and help me with the potatoes and carrots."

"Do we have to?" Lucy groused.

"It's either that or homework and a nap." Christina prepared herself for the expected response.

Lucy's mouth twisted into a grimace. "We aren't babies, Chrissy. Only babies take naps."

"I know quite a few adults who take catnaps in the middle of the afternoon."

Giggling, Lucy's eyes crinkled in delight. "Catnap? Do they sleep with a cat?"

"No, silly," Cici responded. "It just means they sleep for a bit, then wake up. My papa used to do it before..." Her voice trailed off, eyes lowering in sadness.

"Yes, he did, Cici. Papa loved his naps, sometimes taking two or three a day."

Her sad expression disappeared, a smile appearing. "He even snored sometimes."

Lucy laughed at this. "My gramma snored all the time."

"All right, young ladies. It's time to get back to fixing supper."

Hex whittled a small piece of wood as he watched the activities from his chair outside the jail. He balanced on the back legs, his gaze missing none of the goings on in front of him.

Zeke rounded the corner, hair mussed, eyes bloodshot, blinking at the fading late afternoon sun. Lowering himself into a chair, he stared straight ahead.

"What was all the racket earlier?"

Hex studied him, shaking his head before returning his attention to the piece of wood. "You need some strong coffee."

"Had four cups at Ruby's. Hasn't helped much."

"Could be the amount of alcohol you had last night."

A pained smile broke across Zeke's face. "That and no sleep." He waggled his brows before wincing at the pain in his head. "So, what was the noise about?"

"Four wagons came through town. Finn Hanrahan and his family. Bought land south of town and plan to open a saloon. Already made arrangements with Noah."

"We've already got the Dixie, Wild Rose, and Ruby's," Zeke said.

"Which are filled to capacity every Friday and Saturday night. Doesn't matter. Finn's going to open his own in the empty building next to the newspaper."

Hex nodded across and down the street to where the town had helped rebuild the newspaper building after an explosion. The owner and his son had been seriously injured, but were now back to work printing the Splendor Herald.

"Four wagons? Any unmarried women?" Zeke asked.

"Finn has two daughters. He didn't say if they were married, but I don't think so. Why, you looking for a woman?"

"Hell no. Curious is all." It was no secret Zeke had feelings for Francesca O'Reilly, an attorney who came to town with three friends months before. "Is Gabe inside?"

"Talking to a possible deputy. I listened for a bit before coming out here." Hex glanced across the street when a couple of cowboys flew out the doors of the Dixie, landing on the boardwalk. A moment later, Nick Barnett, one of the owners, came out, pointing a shotgun at the two. "Guess we won't be needed."

"What you think of the man Gabe's talking to?"

21

"Says he was a Texas Ranger after the war, then a deputy in Denver. Wears a Colt .45." Hex made a couple cuts on the piece of wood in his hand. "He has a scar on his left cheek. Other than that, I've got no opinion until I see him in action." He continued to watch as Nick waited on the boardwalk while the cowboys mounted their horses. Just as Hex thought the two would be smart and leave, one of them drew his six-shooter, spinning his horse to face Nick.

Hex didn't hesitate, dropping the wood and knife, he drew his gun and ran toward them. When the cowboy raised his arm, Hex aimed and fired. The six-shooter flew from the man's hand to land near Nick's feet.

Hex could hear his scream of pain, not able to reach him before the two wheeled their horses around and rode off. Stopping beside Nick, his gaze wandered over his friend, looking for any sign of blood.

"What happened?" Hex holstered his gun, watching the trail to confirm they didn't return. From what he saw, his bullet blew off the tip of at least one finger.

Nick leaned the shotgun against the railing, brushing dust off his black jacket with a few flicks of his fingers, unruffled at the encounter. "The usual. Too much whiskey and too little common sense."

"Did you recognize them?"

"No. I'll ask the bartender. Maybe Paul knows them." Nick clasped a hand on Hex's back. "Come inside and I'll buy you a drink."

He thought about Lucy at home with Cici and Christina, knowing they'd be expecting him soon. "One drink, then I need to get home to Luce. How's Newt?"

Nick's eyes lit up at the mention of his baby son. "The boy's doing just fine. Suzanne's spending three or four hours each day at the boardinghouse. The rest of the time she's with Newt." He signaled Paul for two whiskeys. "You seem to be doing all right with Lucy." Nick lifted his glass, holding it out to touch the rim of Hex's.

"I wouldn't be able to do it without Chrissy's help."

"You should marry the girl."

Hex choked at Nick's words, setting down his glass to catch his breath. "Marry her? She's still a child herself."

Nick leaned back, studying Hex. "A child? You must be blind. I can tell you none of the men in here would see her as anything except the woman she is." He tossed back his drink, setting the glass down. "The fact is, if the single men knew you only see her as someone to help with Lucy, she'd be buried in offers to court."

"Court..." Hex whispered, finishing what was left of his whiskey.

"It's when a man shows his interest in a woman."

"I know what the hell courting is, Nick."

"Are you sure? Because the meaning seems to have escaped you."

Hex stopped outside the front door of his house, considering again what Nick had said. Her birthday was a few days away. She'd be twenty-one, an age where many women in the frontier were already married. How had he not noticed?

Blowing out a breath, he gripped the knob, hesitating a moment before opening the door. Lucy and Cici played with rag dolls Christina had made them.

"Papa!" His daughter dropped the doll, jumping up to rush into his open arms. It had only been the last month she'd begun calling him papa instead of Hex. He liked the change.

"Luce." He held her in the air, turning in a circle to the sound of her giggles. Holding her against his chest, he kissed her cheek before setting her down.

Removing his hat and gunbelt, he turned toward the kitchen. Christina stood over the stove, stirring their supper. The aroma drew him forward.

He took his time covering the short distance, his gaze roaming over her. Her dress draped over graceful curves, the curves of a woman, just like Nick said.

"Good evening, Hex. Supper's almost ready. Chicken stew, biscuits, and vinegar pie. I'll wait until the biscuits are ready, then Cici and I will leave you two alone."

"Can't you stay and eat with us?" He wanted more time to figure out how he'd missed her transition to a beautiful woman.

"Not tonight. Maybe another time." She smiled, transferring the biscuits to a bowl and covering them with a towel.

"Seems there's plenty here. Won't you reconsider?"

Tilting her head, she studied Hex, wondering at his objection to her leaving. He'd never cared one way or another if she and Cici stayed or left.

"Wish we could, but I've made other plans."

His back stiffened, lips drawing into a thin line. "Meeting someone?"

"What? No, nothing like that, although there is a man who interests me." She wouldn't admit it was Hex.

Forcing himself to relax, he rested a shoulder against the wall. "Care to share his name?"

Christina chuckled, slipping into her coat. "No, I would not. Unless, of course, you want to share the women who interest you."

It was a challenge. He knew it, but wouldn't be drawn into her game. Besides, the only woman he'd been attracted to recently was Alana Hanrahan, and they'd only just met.

"We saw you talking to the people in wagons, Papa." Lucy didn't look up from playing with her doll.

Cici stood, putting her doll in her pocket. "The lady with red hair is real pretty, Hex."

He glanced at Christina, seeing her smile fade before she looked away. "Yes, she is quite beautiful, Hex. So is the nurse who came to town with Francesca O'Reilly."

She mentioned one of the five friends of Rachel Pelletier who'd arrived from New York. Zeke hadn't been able to hide his interest in Francesca, although he'd yet to make a move. Walking to the door, she motioned for Cici to come along. "I'll be here again tomorrow. Enjoy your supper."

"Chrissy, wait."

"Your food will be getting cold. Have a good evening."

Jaw dropping at her quick departure, he wondered at what had caused her to rush away. She and Cici always stayed for supper when he asked.

"I think you should marry Chrissy, Papa."

Settling his hands on his waist, he shifted to look at his daughter. "I'm not looking to marry, Luce."

She stopped playing long enough to glance up at him, her features serious. "You told me Uncle Chan said that before he got married."

Chapter Three

U.S. Marshal Chan Evans strolled into the jail the next morning along with Beth, his wife of a couple months. His brother, Gabe, had hired her as a deputy, an unheard of but popular move. She'd been a secret service agent on a case in Splendor, quitting after she and Chan wed. It was a perfect job for her.

"Any coffee left?" Chan already headed for the stove, filling two cups, handing one to Beth. Taking a sip, he winced. "After all this time, how is it none of you can make a decent cup of coffee?"

His brother, Gabe, leaned back in his chair, crossing his arms. "Father says the same. He's ordered coffee from back east. The same as we use in my New York hotels."

"Expensive," Chan added. "Can you afford it on your budget?"

"No." Gabe chuckled.

He and his family, including Chan, were wealthy. They worked because they loved it, accepting the rough western frontier as home. Chan knew Gabe often used personal funds to supplement the meager amount allowed by the town leaders.

Sitting next to Beth, Chan stretched out his legs, crossing them at the ankles. "Anything exciting happening around here?"

"Nothing, except a large family arrived in four wagons yesterday. Clausen sold them acreage south of town, and Noah rented them the empty building next to the newspaper. They're going to open a saloon."

"How do you feel about that?" Chan and everyone else in town knew Nick and Gabe owned the Dixie and Wild Rose.

"I'm not worried. The town is growing." Gabe glanced at Beth, tempering what he'd been about to say. "Finn plans to offer entertainment we don't."

Chan's reply was interrupted when the door opened, Dax Pelletier entering. Tipping his hat at Beth, he took a chair from against the wall, turning it around to straddle it.

Dax and his brother, Luke, owned the largest cattle ranch in western Montana, raising Herefords and were working with Dom Lucero to crossbreed them with Texas longhorns. Smart, hardworking, and extremely successful, they'd always been the first to help those in need.

"What brings you to town, Dax?"

Removing his hat, he tossed it on the desk, a smile tilting the corners of his mouth. "The boys have been talking about having a competition."

"What kind of competition?" Chan asked before Gabe had the chance.

"Six-shooters and rifles. Luke, Bull, and Dirk have been talking details."

"What about knives?" Gabe cast a look at his brother. Few knew Chan's expertise with knives.

"Don't see why not. They're thinking about putting teams together from the various ranches, and anyone in town who wants to compete. Twelve, if we can get that many interested." Standing, Dax walked to the stove, pouring a cup of coffee. Taking a sip, he winced. "Worst coffee I've ever had, Gabe. Hope this isn't what you serve in your hotels."

Chan, Beth, and Gabe shared a look before bursting out in laughter.

"What?"

Beth swiped a tear from her face. "Chan said the same, Dax. Walter's ordering coffee from back east."

"Out of his own pocket," Chan clarified.

Gabe waved a hand in the air. "Enough about my bad coffee. Let's talk about the competition."

Walking to the back door, Dax tossed out the rest of the coffee, setting the cup on a shelf near the stove. "Teams would be four to five men." He glanced at Beth. "Or women. Several of the women in town can shoot. They can sign on for any of the events. One or all three, or four if we come up with something else. No cost except for ammunition. Luke and I will cover the cost of targets."

"The deputies could spread the word in town," Beth said, warming to the idea. "Maybe the church and school could use it as a fundraiser by selling pies, cakes, and bread. And some games for the children." Her broad smile and enthusiasm stopped the men from objecting.

Chan took his wife's hand, kissing the knuckles. "The entire town could be involved."

Lowering himself back into the chair, Dax wondered what his men would think about the changes. "I don't see a problem with any of it. We'll need to be sure everyone is out of range for the shooting contests."

"When would you want to do this?"

Dax rubbed his chin. "Two weeks. That way, it won't interfere with spring roundup. Does that give us enough time?"

"It will have to be. I'll talk with Lena."

"She's got her hands full with baby Emma, Gabe. Maybe Clare could be put in charge of organizing the women." Dax mentioned his wife, Rachel's aunt. She'd married Doc Worthington more than a year before and had worked hard to become a part of the community.

"She'll be able to get the church women involved," Beth added.

Gabe slapped both hands on the desk before standing. "Two weeks from Saturday. On the outskirts of the south end of town."

"I'll get Cash and Beau to select the site for the contest. The community center is on the town's southern border, which will make it easy to use for the bake sale." Gabe sent a firm look at Dax. "Your boys at the ranch and the town women will have to figure out the rest."

"Fair enough. Good to see you, Beth, Chan. Why don't you come out to the ranch for supper on Friday? We can work on the details."

"Thanks, Dax. We'll be there." Chan shook his hand.

After Dax left, Beth stood, walking to the door. "I'd better get out there." She adjusted her deputy badge. "Do you want to start spreading the word about the contest?"

"Shooting contest *and* community festival, Beth. Two weeks isn't much time to get everything together."

Beth nodded at fellow deputies Hex, Caleb, and Mack when they entered the jail. "I'll speak with Mr. Gibson at the newspaper. Maybe he can print some flyers."

"Flyers for what?" Caleb asked, setting his hat on a hook by the door.

Beth shot a look at her boss. "Gabe will explain. There's a lot to get done and not much time to do it."

"Alana, Brenda." Finn Hanrahan waved them over to where he stood with the other men. "We'll be leaving for town to start work on the saloon. The gaming tables and piano will be arriving in the next few days from Big Pine and we want to be ready."

He'd already hired Noah Brandt and his men to build-out the second floor with individual rooms for *guests*. Finn had explained to his landlord they'd be renting rooms, similar to the boardinghouse in town. It wasn't the complete truth, but in the Irishman's eyes, close enough.

"What do you want us to do while you're gone?" Alana asked. "It's boring in camp." She plopped onto a downed tree trunk, clearly unhappy at being left behind. "Why can't Brenda and I go with you?"

Finn took off his hat, scratching his head. "Hell, girl, you're always bored. Even when singing and dancing, you're unhappy."

Her smile was forced, too bright to be real. "Taking me to town will help. I can let people know we'll be opening soon. Maybe buy a new dress for the first performance."

Brenda stepped to his side. "Me, too, Finn. Dara can stay here with the other women to finish setting up camp."

"Dara's still sleeping," Alana laughed. "Too much whiskey last night. She probably won't even know we're gone until we return."

Finn knew all too well Dara's tendency to spend nights inside a bottle of whiskey and days sleeping it off. "All right, but no dresses. There's no money for additional frivolities."

"We brought in plenty of extra money at the saloon in Denver," Brenda protested.

Jumping up, Alana crossed her arms. "And we didn't get anything for the work."

"You got food, a place to stay, and free drinks. Be happy with it 'cause you're not getting anything more." Finn whirled around, stalking toward the wagon where Dara slept. He could hear her snores from several feet away and stopped. Frustration rolled through him.

The woman he'd fallen in love with at seventeen had become a burden, had been for years. Finn couldn't count the number of years he'd been without a true wife. Given her current health, he didn't expect her to live more than a few months. God help him, he couldn't find it in him to feel an impending sense of loss. The woman he'd married had left him years before.

Jaw clenched, Finn looked over his shoulder at the girls. "If you're expecting to go, you'd better saddle horses. We leave in five minutes."

Scrambling so as not to be left behind, Alana and Brenda grabbed blankets and saddles. Once the bridles were in place, they retrieved bonnets and reticules from the wagon. They were ready five minutes later.

Finn and his brother drove the wagon filled with supplies while everyone else rode on horseback. It was already mid-morning, past time they should've been on the trail.

Their land was closer to town than Finn had realized when he bought it. On a good day, it would take less than an hour to reach Splendor by wagon and thirty minutes by horse. With the rooms above the saloon, they could also stay overnight. He knew Alana and Brenda would make that choice most nights.

Reaching the outskirts of town, he turned the wagon to the left, straight down the main street. Spotting the newspaper building, he drew to a stop before it. He'd paid little attention to it when they'd come through town, not wanting to answer too many questions about the family or business.

Today, they'd unload their supplies and disappear inside. He expected the sheriff, deputies, and the bank manager, Horace Clausen, to come by, but hoped others would stay away. They needed every minute available to get the saloon ready to open as soon as possible.

Hex leaned against a post on the boardwalk, watching the wagon and riders approach. He'd spoken to Noah earlier, learning he and his workers had added rooms upstairs for boarders. Hex didn't believe it.

A boardinghouse would have a kitchen and facilities for travelers. Not this saloon.

Hex wondered what part Alana played in the entertainment Finn planned to offer. From his vantage point on the boardwalk across the street, she looked innocent, not at all the type of woman who would offer her charms for money.

Curiosity and a decent amount of lust gripping him, Hex headed across the street toward the two women still atop their horses. Alana noticed him first, her fetching smile aimed directly at him.

"Good morning, Deputy Boudreaux."

He touched the brim of his hat at both, but his attention fixed on Alana. "Miss Hanrahan. What brings you to town?"

"Papa and the other men need to complete the inside of the saloon so we can open on time." She didn't acknowledge Brenda sliding to the ground, tossing her reins over the hitching post before going inside the cavernous space. "Are you on duty today, Deputy?" Her voice was silky smooth with a slight lilt.

"Yes, ma'am. May I assist you down?" Hex took a step toward her horse, lifting his arms.

"Why, that would be lovely." She held out her hands, settling them on his shoulders. As he set her down, she let them run down his arms, taking her time. "I do so want to see the town. Perhaps you'd have time to show me around?"

Holding out his arm, he tried to ignore the kick to his gut when she slipped hers through it. "It would be my honor, Miss Hanrahan."

"I would appreciate it if you'd call me Alana."

He began strolling toward the St. James Hotel, taking his time. "All right, as long as you call me Hex."

She stayed close to his side, not allowing more than two or three inches between them. "Have you lived in Splendor long?"

"Less than two years."

"Do you intend to stay?"

Hex had wondered the same until he learned about Lucy. As a single father, he welcomed the community who stepped forward to help him, Zeke, and his daughter feel at home.

"Yes. At least for now." He stopped in front of the hotel. "This is the nicest place in town to stay, and the Eagle's Nest is the best restaurant until you reach the Pacific." Perhaps an exaggeration, but not by much, according to Caro Davis and Isabella Dixon, who'd lived in San Francisco for a time.

"The church is ahead. It burned down over a year ago. The town and ranchers came together to rebuild it." Crossing the street, he stopped in front of Allie Coulter's shop.

"Oh, a dress shop." Alana tugged him toward the window, refusing to let go of her hold on his arm. "What beautiful gowns and hats."

"Allie's very talented. She's married to another of the deputies, Cash Coulter. She plans to add more dry goods so local women can purchase their own fabric. That way, they won't have to save for mail order dresses."

Moving on, he walked past the bank, law offices, stopping outside McCall's. "Another good restaurant. Betts Jones serves large helpings, so you need to be hungry when you go inside."

Her stomach growled at the mention of food. "Maybe I'll go in sometime."

Hex looked down at her, making a quick decision. "Would you allow me to buy lunch today? It's a little early, so we can wait if you'd prefer."

Alana felt a stab of triumph, schooling her expression with a warm smile. "I would love to have lunch with you, Deputy. And there's no better time than right now."

Chapter Four

Alana stared at the handsome deputy, pleased with her progress for the day. They'd had an excellent meal, including dessert, and shared conversation, although she was certain her comments weren't nearly as truthful as his.

She found herself wondering about his financial situation, if he owned a house, had savings. "Are you single, Hex?"

Her bold question surprised him. Few women would be so daring as to inquire. Then again, Alana was new to town.

"I live with my brother, also a deputy, and my daughter."

Brows lifting, she choked on a sip of coffee before recovering. "Daughter?"

"Lucy. She's five and a real handful." He studied her over the rim of his cup, waiting for a response.

"Well, that's wonderful. Her mother is?"

"Dead."

"How awful for you." Alana didn't believe a daughter would be a problem with her plans for the deputy. It might even work in her favor.

"So far, we're doing fine." Hex paused, an image of Christina appearing in his mind. Lucy loved her, wanted him to marry her. In truth, he found Christina appealing in many ways. He'd been attracted to her from the time they'd met on the stagecoach from Big Pine. Then why was he having lunch with Alana when he'd never taken Christina anywhere? He looked away, unable to come up with a good answer.

"Is she in school today?"

Glancing out the window, he nodded. "Yes. I have a friend, a woman who works for me, who accompanies her sister and Lucy home each day." *Cleans my house, fixes supper, and entertains the girls,* he didn't add.

As luck would have it, the bell above the door chimed. Christina and Josie Lucero walked in, both stopping at the sight of Hex with a beautiful, young woman. Something passed through him, very much like guilt at being with someone else. Another thought he couldn't explain.

"Hello, Hex," Josie said, her gaze wandering over Alana. "I don't believe we've met."

"Josie, this is Alana Hanrahan, one of the women who came into town with her family yesterday. Alana, this is Josephine Lucero. She owns the emporium across the street. And this is Christina McKenna, the woman I mentioned."

"Oh, yes, your housekeeper and nanny." Alana smiled at the two, a frozen, forced attempt at hospitality that wasn't lost on the others.

Josie choked while Christina gaped between Hex and Alana.

Taking the initiative, Christina waved at Betts, who emerged from the kitchen. "We'll leave you to enjoy your meal." She didn't spare Hex a glance as she moved past him to a table Betts indicated, Josie behind her. Christina chose a chair with her back to the two, feeling as if she'd been slapped.

"What a horrible woman." Josie took a chair facing them, her expression one of unconcealed contempt. "I can't imagine Hex being interested in her."

"He's definitely interested. I saw how he reacted to meeting her yesterday. His tongue all but fell out of his mouth."

Josie burst out laughing, drawing the attention of everyone in the restaurant. After a moment, she drew a handkerchief from her reticule, using it to pat the moisture below her eyes.

"Whatever his infatuation is with the woman, it won't last. If what she said is an example of her manners, Hex will figure it out soon enough."

Christina wished it were true, but would put no stock in it. Men fell for young, lively women all the time. Hex didn't have to marry the woman to spend his free time with her. After all, Christina filled his need for a *housekeeper and nanny*, as the woman had said. He didn't need to marry to get everything he wanted without making a commitment.

"Would you rather leave? We can walk to the boardinghouse for lunch."

Stiffening her spine, Christina shook her head. "Absolutely not. I can ignore them just fine. When we're done, it will be time to fetch the girls from school."

"You never mentioned how you feel about Hex, but I know you care for him a great deal. Maybe you should stop taking care of his needs at the house and only watch the girls. He'll understand soon enough what he's lost."

"Not if Miss Hanrahan is ready to fill the void." Ordering their food, Christina sat back in the chair. "But I am going to rent the empty house next to Travis and Isabella. I will be able to take the girls there after school instead of watching them at his house."

Josie's face broke into a mischievous grin. "Perfect, and the sooner the better. He'll lose his free housekeeper, cook, and laundress. It will also signal the other single men in town that you're available."

Christina took in her words, knowing her friend was right. It was time she put distance between her and Hex, allowing both to meet others who might interest them. Allow Christina to be courted.

She wondered what he would think of changing their arrangement. Would he even care if she wasn't available for doing work he took for granted. Glancing over her shoulder at the scrape of the chair across the wood floor, her heart squeezed. She couldn't move from the boardinghouse and into her new home soon enough.

41

Hex's stomach roiled, throat tightening. Christina's face had paled at Alana's comment. She was his friend, dedicated to his family, and he'd done nothing to correct Alana's impression. He had a lot to make up for, assuming she decided to continue helping with Lucy.

Standing, he placed money on the table. Walking behind Alana's chair, he thought of how he'd get himself out of this mess. Then he considered why it mattered.

There were other women who'd be happy to help with Lucy. If Christina decided to quit after the comment, that was her choice. He'd survive.

Holding out his arm for Alana, he didn't glance at the table where Josie and Christina sat before stepping outside.

"She is quite lovely, Hex. And she's interested in you." Alana had learned at a young age not to curb her words.

"What? No, she's a friend, nothing more." As the words left his lips, he knew they were a lie. She was more than a friend, and she'd been hurt.

"That's good, because I've already decided I want you interested only in *me*."

Again, she'd shocked him. Hex didn't respond, not wanting to dig the hole any deeper.

She snuggled next to him, quite pleased with the way their lunch had ended.

Walking her back to the unfinished saloon, he disengaged himself and stepped away. "Thank you for joining me for lunch, Alana."

"It was completely my pleasure, Deputy." Lifting her hand, she ran it down the lapel of his coat. "I hope to see you again...soon."

"Hey, Hex."

He looked up, seeing Caleb waving at him from in front of the Dixie. "Gabe's inside and wants to speak with you."

Relief flooded him. "On my way. I'll be going now, Alana." He touched the brim of his hat, turning away.

It wasn't the reply she'd expected. "Shall I see you opening night?"

Stopping for a brief moment, he glanced over his shoulder. "I'll do my best."

Stalking down the boardwalk, Hex felt conflicted. He didn't know if Alana had any idea how her words had affected Christina. From what he'd told her, Christina did function as his housekeeper and nanny, he'd just never thought of her in those terms.

Either way, it hurt Christina, which wasn't right. His thoughts of earlier, that she shouldn't take the comments personally, were ridiculous. A woman with a gracious nature and big heart shouldn't have to endure such senseless comments, even if unintended.

Heading into the Dixie, he put thoughts of both women behind him. He had a lot of thinking to do.

"You wanted to see me, Gabe?"

The sheriff leaned against the bar, talking with Nick. "I wanted to make sure you and Caleb knew about the shooting contest and community festival the town is talking about."

"I've heard nothing about either one," Caleb replied while Hex shook his head.

Gabe explained what the Pelletier ranch hands planned. "I'd like you and the other deputies to spread the word. Maybe form your own shooting team."

"You want to be on it, Sheriff?" Caleb asked.

Chuckling, Gabe shook his head. "Hell no. I'd only hold you boys back. I intend for you to do the office proud."

The deputies consisted mostly of ex-military with experience in law enforcement elsewhere. All were competent shooters, some considered expert.

"We have enough deputies for one team, with the rest watching the crowd and keeping the drunks away." Gabe looked at Nick. "Maybe we shouldn't sell liquor the day of the contest."

Tapping fingers on the bar, Nick shook his head. "Might cause more of a ruckus. You know how those cowboys are on Saturday. It's their one day to cut loose. We could hire men to guard the doors, not let anyone near the contest if they've been drinking."

"Probably the best you can do, Gabe." Hex rubbed the back of his neck, still unable to erase Alana and Christina from his mind.

One, a vibrant, outspoken woman who'd undoubtedly seen more of the world than he wanted to believe. The other, a devoted sister who never complained, always offering a caring hand. One, self-centered, on the search for fun. The other, educated, humble, a woman you could spend years getting to know.

Thinking of them in those terms, there really was no choice which was the better woman for him. Then why did he sense such a growing desire for Alana?

His father had said there were two kinds of women. One you played around with, the other you offered your heart. Hex had no doubt which was which.

"Hex, do you want to organize the deputy team with Caleb? You are two of our best shooters."

Gabe's voice drew him from his thoughts. "Sure, Sheriff. How many are we talking about per team?"

"Dax mentioned four or five."

Caleb shrugged. "No problem. We'll take care of it. Anything else we can do?"

"Spreading the word and organizing a team is all. Two weeks from Saturday, beyond the south end of town."

Hex gave a mock salute. "Yes, sir. Unless there's anything else, I'll be going."

Stepping into the still warm afternoon, his gaze roamed the street. He didn't want to run into Alana again today.

Looking the other direction, he did spot three figures he recognized, his heart warming. His daughter, Lucy, was heading home from school with Cici and Christina.

Stepping into the shadows of the boardwalk, he remained silent, not wanting to draw anyone's attention. They walked down the main street, stopping at the general store. A few minutes later, Christina walked out, carrying a burlap bag. The girls followed, each sucking on a piece of peppermint candy.

Laughing at something Lucy said, they retraced their steps, turning just past the general store on their way to Hex's house. When he got home in two hours, the house would be clean, girls playing, and supper cooking. As Zeke would say, his life was idyllic, one any man would crave. Why today did it seem so empty?

Chapter Five

Shoving open the door of Hex's house, Christina ushered the girls inside. "Do you have lessons for tonight?"

"Only a little, Chrissy," Cici answered, running behind Lucy to the girl's bedroom.

"Finish your peppermint sticks, then get your studies done. Afterward, you can play outside for a while. Or you can help me with supper." She held her breath, not waiting long.

"Outside," both girls shouted.

Today, she wouldn't ask more of them. Christina needed time to think. After lunch, she'd visited Noah at the livery, finalizing plans to move into the house next to Isabella and Travis. She'd already told Suzanne about moving out of the boardinghouse. Noah had offered the use of his wagon, which she graciously accepted. There wasn't much to transfer. A couple trunks filled with clothing, books, and blankets. A satchel with personal papers, cards, stationary, a wood chair, table, and kerosene lamp.

There was furniture still in the family home in Kansas City. They owned the house and land free and clear, as well as everything in it. She and Millicent had planned to have their belongings shipped to a new home on the Pacific. Christina would now ship them to Splendor, part going into the small home, the rest stored in a building Noah and Abby owned on the outskirts of town. One day, she hoped to marry, move everything into a large home with her husband, Cici, and the children they planned.

Instead of the dream of her future giving her hope, today, it saddened her. Over the time she'd worked for Hex, Christina had convinced herself the taciturn lawman would fall in love with her, as she had with him. Seeing him today, the dream began to fade.

Having her own house would help put distance between them. She'd still watch the girls, but instead of making supper and waiting for Hex to return to his place, they'd be at her house. Christina already had her reasoning planned, rehearsed it after leaving lunch with Josie to fetch the girls.

Removing the beef roast purchased from the meat market that morning, she rubbed it with salt and pepper. Placing it in a roasting pan with some water, she slid it into the oven compartment of the wood stove.

She counted out six potatoes, enough for Hex, Zeke, and Lucy. Cleaning and cutting them, she set the chunks aside, covering them with a cloth. It had become her habit to fix herself tea while cleaning and waiting for supper to cook. Today, she sat down, an odd mixture of excitement and despair claiming her.

In a few days, she and Cici would be venturing into another new chapter of their lives. They'd sew curtains, make pillows, and have their own bedrooms, maybe a garden out back. Sipping her tea, she made a mental list of what she had to accomplish to make the house their home.

Realizing it had been too long since she'd heard the girls, Christina looked out the window to the side yard. The girls were playing in the dirt. She didn't have the energy to scold them for their choice of activity or dirtying their clothes, she stepped away. There'd be time to clean them up before Hex returned home.

The sound of the front door opening had her whirling around. Instead of Hex, Zeke strolled in, tossing his hat on a nearby table, scanning the room while listening. "Afternoon, Chrissy. The girls around?"

"Playing outside. Don't worry, I'll get them cleaned up before Hex arrives."

"Hey, I don't care how dirty they get. As long as they're happy..." He walked to the stove, pouring a cup of coffee. Holding up the pot, he held it toward her.

"No, thank you. I'm drinking tea."

Zeke visibly shuttered. "I don't know how you can drink that weak stuff. A man needs something strong."

"I know, but some days, tea is all I want."

"Smells good in here. You two staying for supper?"

"Not tonight."

Zeke leaned against the counter, sipping the coffee. "That's two nights in a row. Did one of us say something to offend you?"

A small smile tipped her lips. "Not at all. I just think the three of you should be able to have a quiet supper alone."

"Don't forget Saturday night."

She glanced up, brows drawing together.

"We're taking you to supper at the boardinghouse to celebrate your birthday."

Rubbing her brow, Christina winced. She didn't want to spend more time than necessary around Hex, but couldn't turn down such a thoughtful invitation.

"I remember. Just didn't realize Saturday was a couple days away. Cici and I are looking forward to it. And, Zeke, thank you both for thinking of me."

Setting down his cup, he studied her, seeing uncommon wrinkles around her eyes and the corners of her mouth. "Are you feeling all right, Chrissy?"

"A little tired, but fine." Pushing herself up, she checked the roast. "It's browning nicely." Adding the potatoes, she slid it back inside, closing the door. "It'll be ready when Hex gets here. Do you mind if I take Cici back to the boardinghouse?"

"If you're certain you can't stay. I know Hex would like to see you."

She snorted, removing her apron and hanging it on a hook. "Believe me, Hex won't even notice I'm not here. Do you want me to send Lucy inside? I can stay and get her cleaned up."

"You two go on ahead. I'll take care of Lucy."

Standing next to the back door, Zeke watched her from the window. Something was wrong. *Very* wrong. None of the easy banter. No warm smile. Nothing of the usual Christina.

Hex stepped through the front door, hearing the quiet. Zeke sat at the table with Lucy, her reading primer in front of her. He didn't disturb them.

Placing his hat and gunbelt on hooks by the door, he lowered himself into a leather overstuffed chair. The one splurge he'd made since he and Zeke had arrived in Splendor. His brother had spent any extra money he had on a beautiful pair of hand tooled boots he'd spotted in Big Pine.

Other than those purchases, the Boudreaux brothers saved their pennies and invested. They hoped to buy a small ranch in a few years, keeping their jobs in town. There was a place south of town they'd been watching for months. Not large enough for most ranchers, but the perfect size for two deputies who wanted to raise a small herd and keep a few horses.

It did have a house perched on a rise, with a view north and west. Two stories with four bedrooms and a wraparound porch would be perfect for the three of them. Large enough if one or both ever married, and room to expand.

He watched his daughter and brother, heads together, as they worked through some difficult words. After a couple minutes, Lucy looked up, noticing him for the first time.

"Papa!" Jumping down from the chair, she ran into his open arms. "What took you so long?"

Chuckling, he settled her on his lap. "Did you miss me?"

Wrinkling her nose, Lucy kissed his cheek, then squirmed off his lap to the floor. "Chrissy and Cici went home."

She'd answered the question he was about to ask. He looked at Zeke, who shrugged. "I asked them to stay." Zeke looked at Lucy. "We need a few sticks of wood. How about you gather them for us?"

Groaning, she made a show of stalking out the back door, leaving the two men alone.

"What's going on with Chrissy?"

Zeke's question caught Hex by surprise. "What do you mean?" He already suspected what bothered her, hoping he was wrong.

"She wasn't her usual self. Chrissy always has a smile, enjoys talking while fixing supper. Today, well...maybe she's not feeling well."

Hex didn't believe that was the case. "Did she mention her birthday supper at Suzanne's?"

"She and Cici plan to be there, although she didn't seem real excited about it."

Hex knew exactly what bothered her and believed he held some responsibility for it. Alana had been out of line at McCall's, and Chrissy was too gracious to correct her. He and Zeke paid her a little each day to fetch Lucy from school and watch her until Hex returned from work. Making them supper and cleaning had been her decision. Even so, they always added a little money for the extra work.

She was *not* their housekeeper or nanny. Chrissy was a good friend who offered her help. At least he'd considered her a friend until the calamity today. If only he'd stood up for her, corrected Alana's assumption.

The worst of it was Hex had known for a while how Chrissy felt about him. She may not love him, but cared a great deal. He'd done his best to ignore what he considered her infatuation with him until Alana arrived in town. It took the woman throwing herself at him for Hex to evaluate his feelings for Chrissy.

To his shock, they ran much deeper than he realized. Now he had to decide what, if anything, to do about it.

"Do you have any idea what's going through her pretty head?" Zeke asked when Hex remained silent for several minutes.

"I might." Standing, he headed to the kitchen, opening a cupboard to pull down the bottle of whiskey on the top shelf. Pouring a small amount into a slender glass receptacle, he tossed it back. "I invited Alana Hanrahan to have lunch with me."

Zeke sat up straighter. "One of the women who arrived in town this week?"

Hex nodded. "Chrissy came into McCall's with Josie." His mouth twisted into a grimace. "Alana said something Chrissy took exception to, made a wrong assumption about her work for us. As usual, Chrissy handled it with her usual class, but I knew the comment hurt her."

"I'm guessing you didn't say anything to correct what Alana said."

Hex hated the way Zeke knew him so well. "No, I didn't."

Pouring a little more whiskey into the glass, he swallowed it in one gulp as Lucy returned, her arms laden with sticks of firewood. "Thank you, sweetheart."

Dropping it on top of the pile by the stove, she picked up a few pieces, adding them to the firebox. "Chrissy made roast with potatoes." Rubbing her stomach, she sent a pleading look at her father. "Can we eat now?"

"We sure can." Hex pulled down plates. "Wash up before setting the table."

She stuck out her lower lip, but did what he said before a smile lit her face. "Do we really get to go to Suzanne's for Chrissy's birthday supper?"

"We sure do," Hex answered.

He'd ordered a special cake from May Covington, Caleb's wife and pastry chef at Eagle's Nest. Sweet and kind, she'd been thrilled to be asked, already knowing what she'd bake.

Transferring the roast and potatoes to the table where Zeke still sat, he motioned for Lucy to join him. Hex pulled out a chair, clasping his hands together and bowing his head. His brother and daughter followed his lead, waiting as he said a short prayer. Serving all three, he sat back as the other two dug in.

"I do believe Chrissy is one of the best cooks in town." Zeke chewed a succulent piece of roast, stabbing another. "Wish they would've stayed to eat with us. Even the incident with Alana shouldn't have made Chrissy leave."

"What happened, Uncle Zeke?" Lucy stared at him, her mouth tipping into a frown.

Grimacing, he sent an apologetic look at Hex. "Nothing important, sweetheart."

But Hex wasn't paying attention. His mind was on a beautiful woman he realized had begun to mean a great deal to him. A woman he truly wanted to know better.

Chapter Six

Chrissy fiddled with the ruffled collar of her new dress, wanting to look perfect for her birthday supper. After tonight, Hex and Zeke would know of her renting the house next to Isabella, her desire to watch the girls there instead of at their home. She told herself it was a wise decision.

The time had come for her and Cici to have their own place instead of living in the cramped quarters at the boardinghouse. It had been a godsend when they'd first arrived in Splendor with an ailing Millie. The three had stayed in the same room, Suzanne providing a small cot for Cici.

This evening, her younger sister sat in the corner, reading from her primer. She'd already dressed, taking no more than fifteen minutes to rush through the ritual of preparing for supper downstairs. Christina took longer, her mind switching between tonight and the move to their new place tomorrow. Checking the time on the watch pendant pinned to her dress, she lifted two shawls from the coat tree.

"Are you ready, Cici?"

The nine-year-old's head slowly rose from where it had been buried in the book. "Do you think they're here yet?"

"There's one way to find out." Chrissy held out the smaller shawl to Cici. "If they aren't, we'll wait for them at the table."

Jumping to the floor, she grabbed the shawl from her sister's outstretched hand. "Do you think Hex and Zeke will have a present for you?"

Chuckling at the foolish notion, Chrissy shook her head. "Supper is more than I expected. A gift would be too much."

"But you like gifts." She swung the shawl over her shoulders, halting at the knock on their door.

"Chrissy, it's Suzanne. Hex, Zeke, and Lucy are downstairs."

Cici pulled the door open, a grin spreading from ear to ear. "We're ready."

Suzanne stayed in the hall, peering into their room. "Don't you look lovely."

"Chrissy bought it for me this morning at the general store." She twirled around, the skirt billowing around her.

"It's perfect, Cici, as is Chrissy's dress."

"I bought it from Allie Coulter. Do you think the color looks good on me?"

"The emerald is wonderful with your strawberry blonde hair and green eyes, Chrissy. Hex is going to swallow his own tongue."

"Whether he does or not doesn't matter. He's interested in one of the new women who came into town last week. Alana Hanrahan."

Suzanne leaned against the doorframe, features softening. "If so, she won't hold his interest for long. Nick believes they'll stay in town long enough to fleece people, then move on."

Chrissy draped the shawl over her shoulders, brows knitting together. "I heard they bought land south of town."

Suzanne shook her head and snorted. "Nick spoke with Horace Clausen at the bank. He's never heard of them, but the land could've been sold to them by a banker in Big Pine. The family who abandoned it didn't use the Bank of Splendor. Clausen is sending a telegram to Sheriff Parker Sterling to find out more about them."

"What about the saloon?" Chrissy's head swam with the possible ramifications if the family lied about purchasing the land.

"The building is owned by Noah and Abby Brandt. Clausen says they rented it to Finn Hanrahan."

"But Nick doesn't trust them." Chrissy drew the shawl more closely around her.

"Not at all. He plans to talk to Gabe. They're going to wait for Clausen to hear back from Parker in Big Pine. For now, don't believe anything they say." Straightening, Suzanne motioned toward the stairs. "You two should be getting downstairs. Don't want to keep two eligible men waiting."

Giggling, Cici took off ahead of them, hurrying down the stairs.

"Slow down," Chrissy called, knowing it was too late. By now, Cici would already be at their table.

Suzanne walked beside her down the stairs. "Are you ready for the move tomorrow?"

"We don't have much, so it won't take long to pack. Noah is bringing his wagon in the morning."

"If you need any help, send Cici to get me."

Touching Suzanne's arm, Chrissy offered a grateful smile. "Thank you, but you should spend Sunday with Nick and Newt. We'll do fine. If needed, I'm certain Hex and Zeke would help."

"Of course they will. Perhaps you can mention what I told you about the Hanrahans."

Chrissy's mouth twisted as she thought about saying anything unflattering about Alana. She had no doubt Hex would dismiss it as her being upset about what the woman had said at McCall's.

"I'll let Gabe tell his deputies about what they learn."

"Understandable." Suzanne nodded to the dining room. "They're waiting for you. I'd better get back into the kitchen." When Chrissy turned to leave, she touched her arm. "Give Hex a little time. He's a smart man. It won't take him long to figure out Alana isn't the woman he wants."

She watched Suzanne return to the kitchen. "I may not be what he wants, either," Chrissy mumbled to herself as she walked toward their table.

Her heart skipped several beats when Hex stood, a bright smile of welcome on his face.

"There's the birthday gal." He pulled out her chair, brushing a chaste kiss across her cheek, causing her breath to hitch. Hex had never shown any amount of intimacy. What he'd done would be considered inappropriate by most people.

Chrissy felt her face flush as she took the chair he offered, sitting next to Lucy. "Thank you for inviting us to supper." She had a hard time meeting his gaze, choosing to look at Zeke and Lucy.

"How old are you, Chrissy?" Lucy asked, earning low chuckles from the two men.

"You aren't supposed to ask that, Lucy." Cici giggled, putting a hand over her mouth.

Seeing the stricken look on the young girl's face, Chrissy touched her shoulder. "I'm twenty-one, Lucy." She chanced a glance at Hex, seeing nothing indicating surprise. So he knew her age and still chose to see her as much younger, unsuitable for a more worldly man. Quite unlike how he saw Alana.

Taking his seat on the other side of her, Hex found it hard to tear his gaze away from her beautiful face. He succeeded when Suzanne approached the table.

"Is everyone ready to eat?"

Lucy spoke first. "I am."

"Me, too," Cici said.

Suzanne looked at Hex, who nodded. "I'll be right back with your food."

They spoke of inconsequential topics while eating steak with potatoes from Delmonico's. Suzanne had gotten the recipe from Gary Werth, the head chef at Eagle's Nest, who'd once worked for what most considered the best restaurant east of the Mississippi.

Conversation stalled when Suzanne brought out a slice of Dutch Apple cake for each of them. "May Covington made this special for you, Chrissy."

"It looks wonderful. I'll have to go by the Eagle's Nest to thank her."

Before anyone picked up their fork, Hex stood. "Happy birthday to a very special lady. We look forward to many more suppers like this one, Chrissy."

The girls clapped while Zeke let out a low whistle. "I'm liking this, Chrissy. We need to do this for each one of us on our birthdays."

"Can we, Papa?" Lucy's eyes lit in excitement.

Hex glanced at Chrissy, wishing she'd talked more that night. She'd been much too quiet, the vivacious, always joyful woman had disappeared. In her place was someone he didn't recognize, a woman whose forced smiles had begun to irritate him.

"Maybe, Luce."

"I have some news." Chrissy turned her attention to Zeke.

He set down his glass. "I hope it's good news."

"I believe it is. Tomorrow, Cici and I are moving into the vacant house next to Isabella." When neither man spoke, she continued. "It will make it easier to watch the girls at my place. When Hex is finished, he can come to my place and get her." She shifted in her chair, feeling Hex's gaze bore into her.

"Are you certain that's what you want?" Zeke asked, tapping fingers on the tabletop.

"Yes, it is. I'll still make supper for you. I have plenty of pots, so you can take it to your place, or the girls and I can carry it over each evening. I'll leave enough for Cici and me." Swallowing the last of her coffee, she set the cup down. "What do you think?"

"I don't like it." Hex's swift, hard response jolted her.

"Why not?"

He seemed to struggle with a response, his mouth drawing into a thin line. "Is this why you haven't had supper with us the last two nights?"

"I've been thinking about making the move for a while, Hex. I wanted to go ahead with it before Noah rented the house to someone else." She'd said it, told the truth without spelling out the exact reason.

Jaw clenched, his gaze narrowed on her. He didn't like her living alone. The boardinghouse offered safety in the numbers of boarders each night. "Is it because of what happened at McCall's?"

Back stiffening, she let out a breath, trying to convey her confusion. "McCall's?"

Hex stared at her. Deciding it best to let it go for now, he drank the rest of his whiskey, features softening.

"Please forget what I said, Chrissy. If moving into your own house is what you want, then tell us how we can help."

Chrissy relaxed, realizing he wasn't going to try to talk her out of it. "Noah is bringing a wagon to the boardinghouse tomorrow after church. I could use help moving the trunks to the house."

"Whatever you need, we'll be there." Zeke turned at the sound of the front door opening, boots sounding on the wood floor. They were masked and nothing about their clothes or stance was family. What he did spot was how each wore dual guns strapped low on their waists. Glancing at Hex, his stern features and stiff posture told Zeke his brother had noticed the same.

Before they could push away from the table, allowing better access to their revolvers, the men made their move. Seconds after entering, the men stormed toward the back of the restaurant, drawing their six-shooters and firing.

A man at a table of five stood, aiming at the men before letting out a blood curdling roar before blooms of red spread across his chest.

Screams filled the air, men and women dropping to the floor to hide under their tables. The men continued to fire, riddling the already dead man's body with bullets.

One of them held up a hand, balling it into a fist. The other two stopped shooting, whirling around to face those in the room, when the leader spoke.

"We're going to back out of here. If anyone moves, it'll mean the death of everyone in here." He didn't wait for a response before they fled the building, the door slamming behind them.

Chapter Seven

Hex drew his weapon, looking over his shoulder at the body lying face down on the table, blood seeping from bullet wounds to his arms, chest, and stomach. Turning to block their view, his gaze moved over the girls, landing on Christina.

"Take Lucy and Cici upstairs and stay there."

Christina nodded, shepherding the girls out of the room and to the second floor.

Zeke pulled his weapon, turning toward the other diners. "Everyone stay inside and away from the windows."

An older woman with gray hair, sallow complexion, and sagging features stared at the body. "Is he dead?"

"Yes, ma'am," Zeke answered. "We'll send the undertaker once we check with the sheriff. He or one of us will come back to talk to you." He nodded at Hex, signaling for both to head outside.

Stepping outside and glancing around, they hurried along the boardwalk before crossing the street to the jail. "Did you recognize anything about them?" Hex asked, keeping his gun in front of him.

"The one man's voice sounded familiar." Zeke cursed. "Not much to go on."

"Whoever they are, they've disappeared. We need to talk to Gabe and the others," Hex said, his gaze still searching the street.

Before they reached the jail, deputies Cash Coulter and Beau Davis ran toward them. "Did you hear gunfire?" Cash turned in a circle, his gun aimed in front of him.

Holstering his six-shooter, Hex nodded at the boardinghouse. "Three men entered the restaurant, shot one of the diners, and fled. Chrissy and the girls are upstairs. We ordered the others to stay in the restaurant. We need to get the undertaker to remove the body."

Beau slid his gun into its holster, taking another look around. "I'll fetch him."

"I'll get Gabe." Cash shifted, speaking to Hex and Zeke when Beau walked down the street. "You two talk to the people inside. Maybe one of them recognized the shooters. We need the identity of the dead man and all those in the restaurant. Do you know if he's a local?"

Hex shook his head. "I've never seen him before tonight."

"Same with me," Zeke said. "If the other diners don't have information on him, I'll check with Suzanne, and at the St. James. Those are the only places he could've stayed, unless he has family in the area."

"If you don't learn anything, try Ruby's Palace. She sometimes allows boarders."

Zeke gave a quick nod at Cash. "I'll do that."

Hex and Zeke headed back to the restaurant while Cash left to find Gabe. Entering the boardinghouse, they found the diners huddled in a back corner,

Suzanne handing out cups of coffee. The body still lay on the table, although someone had thrown a tablecloth over it.

Hex motioned toward chairs. "Everyone take a seat. We need to speak with all of you."

"Why can't we leave?" The older woman from earlier glared at them. "I don't want to stay here with, well...that." She pointed toward the body.

"You'll be able to leave once we've gotten what we need." Hex pulled out a chair, indicating for the woman to sit down.

Instead of questioning them individually, Hex addressed the group. "Who knows the deceased?"

A slender, somewhat older man, fingering his black top hat, cleared his throat. "His name is...I mean, was...Henry Steed. He joined our table, but none of us had met him before tonight."

Hex noticed the others nod in confirmation. "Not one of you met him before tonight?"

A young man in a black suit coated in trail dust spoke up. "I had a drink with him at the Dixie before supper, but didn't get his name. I'm the one who motioned him to our table when he came in here alone. The rest of us arrived on the stage from Cheyenne this afternoon."

"Are you traveling together?" Zeke asked.

The younger man nodded at the older woman. "My aunt and I are going to San Francisco."

The man with the top hat placed his hand over the fourth person, a young woman with dark brown hair and freckles. "My niece and I are also traveling to San Francisco."

Hex studied the four. Something didn't feel right, but he had no idea what. "Was Mr. Steed in the stage with you?"

While the others shook their heads, the younger man spoke. "No. He rode into town alone. Mentioned he'd been through Salt Lake City. At least that's what he said." He shoved his hands into the pockets of his pants. "Wish I'd learned more about him."

"You've given us some good information. If you think of anything else, come by the jail and talk to any of the deputies." Hex sent his brother a meaningful look. "I need to check on Lucy."

"I'll stay down here until the undertaker leaves with Steed's body. Any reason the others need to stay?"

Hex shook his head. "Get their names and find out if they have rooms here or at the St. James before they leave."

Zeke lowered his voice. "Something doesn't seem right about all this."

Hex motioned for his brother to follow him to the stairs. "They aren't telling us the truth."

"No, they aren't."

"Are you certain you don't mind if Lucy stays here a while longer?" Hex continued to hold Lucy, who'd run into his arms the instant Christina opened the door to her and Cici's room.

"Do you have to go, Papa?"

He looked into Lucy's haunted eyes, his gut clenching at the fear he saw. "It won't be for long, sweetheart. Until I speak with Gabe, I need to know you're safe and not alone."

Tightening her hold around her father, Lucy gave a slow nod. "All right." Dropping her arms, she swiped tears from her face.

Crouching in front of his daughter, Hex smiled. "You aren't in any danger, Luce. The bad men are gone and we'll probably never see them again."

"But they killed a man, Papa."

"I know, and we will try to find them."

"Chrissy could draw a picture of the men."

Hex drew away, looking at Chrissy as he stood. "You draw?"

Lucy ran to a bookshelf, grabbing a sketchbook before jumping onto the bed and opening it.

"Luce, I don't think your father would be interested in my drawings."

Hex sat down next to his daughter, staring at the pages as she flipped from one drawing to the next. "These are excellent, Chrissy." He smiled at the almost lifelike drawings of Cici and Lucy. She caught their expressions perfectly.

"Look at these, Papa."

He stilled when Lucy pointed to several images of him. Staring at the stark likeness, he shot her a questioning glance, saying nothing.

When Lucy got to the last drawing, Hex's mouth tipped into a grin. "This woman looks familiar." He glanced up, stifling a chuckle.

Face heating from embarrassment, she lifted the book from Lucy's hands, holding it against her chest. The image showed Alana, her features screwed into a grimace, tiny horns emerging from her head.

"I shouldn't have drawn it. It was...unkind." Setting the book back on the shelf, she sat next to Cici on the small settee, unable to meet Hex's narrowed gaze.

"I should've said something to change her impression of what you do for us, Chrissy. I'm sorry she hurt you."

How could she tell Hex it wasn't Alana's words so much as his letting her believe she was their hired cook and nanny? It wouldn't have mattered if Chrissy felt nothing for him. But she did have strong feelings for the taciturn lawman and single father. She'd already accepted her emotions concerning Hex were one-sided.

"Please don't worry about it. She truly is beautiful, and I'm certain a wonderful companion for you."

He opened his mouth to correct her, grunting in annoyance at the knock on the door.

"It's Suzanne. Gabe is downstairs. He wants to speak with Hex."

Rising, he bent down to kiss Lucy's forehead. "I'll be back as soon as I can."

"She's welcome to stay with us tonight, Hex." Standing, she clasped her hands in front of her.

Opening the door, he stopped, glancing back at her. "I'd prefer Lucy be home with me tonight. I'm sorry about your birthday supper being ruined, Chrissy."

"It was wonderful. Best birthday I've had in a long time."

Gabe shared a table with Zeke, waiting for Hex to join him in the dining room. The undertaker had arrived, loaded the body, and left, followed by the four patrons. Still shaken, they informed Gabe they'd be leaving on the next day's stage.

He'd dashed their plans, explaining they'd be staying in Splendor until he spoke to them again. Gabe sipped coffee, looking up when Hex pulled out a chair. "Something feels wrong about their story."

Zeke stared across the room at the open space where the table had sat. He and Gabe had taken it outside until Suzanne made arrangements to have it cleaned, sanded, and refinished. The same would have to be done to the wood floor. It was her priority. They knew she'd work into the night to clean the space before people arrived for breakfast the next morning.

"How are Chrissy and the girls, Hex?" Gabe leaned forward, resting his arms on the table.

"As well as you'd expect. I agree about the story the stage passengers are telling. It's as if they'd practiced what they'd say." He looked at Zeke. "Do you think the dead man rode in with them?"

"Might've. I didn't pay them a lot of attention, but it seemed they knew him better than they want to admit. Especially the younger man. He mentioned meeting him earlier today, but my instincts tell me he was lying."

"What do you mean?" Gabe asked.

Zeke lifted one shoulder in a shrug. "He wouldn't look me in the eyes, his lips twitched, and he kept sweeping his gaze over the others."

Hex nodded. "And he kept swiping at his face to remove the sweat."

"Then again, they were scared. Could be I'm imagining it all." Zeke pushed from the table and stood. "Do you want me to post myself at the St. James to make sure they don't try to leave town tonight?"

Gabe's mouth twisted, humor in his eyes. "I doubt they'll be going anywhere. They don't have a wagon or horses, and the livery is closed for the night. I do want them at the jail while the stage is in town tomorrow. It needs to leave without them."

"I can watch them," Hex volunteered.

"Tomorrow is Sunday, your day off. Take time with Lucy. It wouldn't surprise me if she has nightmares for a while. I've got enough men to watch the travelers, including a new deputy who'll arrive Monday."

Both men looked at Gabe. "Who?" Hex asked.

Standing, Gabe shoved his hat on his head. "Hawke DeBell."

Chapter Eight

Hex's eyes widened before narrowing on Gabe as he followed him out of the boardinghouse. His mind drew upon the stories he'd heard of the soldier from Georgia. The Confederate captain had a ruthless reputation, who pressed ahead, taking few prisoners during the war.

Afterward, the rumors were he returned to his farm to find the graves of his wife and children. He'd grieved his losses by going after anyone appearing on a wanted poster who could've played a part in their deaths.

"The bounty hunter?"

"The same. Cash and Beau fought with him during the war. They assured me his reputation is more fantasy than fact." Crossing the street toward the jail, Gabe stayed vigilant, hand resting on his six-shooter. "He's ready for a change, at least for a while. However long he stays in Splendor will benefit us."

Hex glanced at Zeke, reading each other's thoughts. From what they knew of the hardened soldier, he would benefit them, although neither expected him to stay long. He was a man with a past which precluded him from finding solace in a life after the war. After the deaths of his family.

"Zeke, you work with Cash and Beau, making extra rounds of town. Hex, get the hell back to the boardinghouse and get your daughter. She needs you more than I do right now."

Hex stared after Gabe and Zeke as they continued to the jail. Lucy was his first priority. She could stay with Christina and Cici, but knew the five-year-old needed her father.

Reversing direction, he returned to the boardinghouse, taking the stairs two at a time. He saw no sign of a light under the door. Hesitating, he tapped, surprised when the door drew open.

The sight of her in bedclothes covered by a thin wrapper had his mouth going dry, his mind stalling for a moment. "Hope I didn't wake you." By her quick response to his knock, he already knew that wasn't the case.

She shook her head. "I was reading. Cici and Lucy are asleep. You're welcome to leave her here for the night."

Hex glanced inside, spotting the young girls sleeping next to each other on the bed. "You need your rest and won't get it curled up on a chair."

Pulling the door wide, she stepped aside for him to enter. "I'll get her coat."

Tugging the covers off Lucy, Hex lifted her into his arms, his heart squeezing. Every day, the love he felt for his daughter had grown a little more, until he didn't realize how he'd lived without her in his life.

Lucy gave him purpose, a view of the future, which had been fuzzy before they were united. Even Zeke had changed since living with his niece. The world through her eyes was so different from those of two jaded ex-soldiers.

Taking the coat from Christina's outstretched hand, he placed it over Lucy. "Thank you. Zeke and I will be back tomorrow to help you move."

"If you're sure it isn't an imposition."

Hex watched a moment, studying the lines at the corners of her eyes, the way she wouldn't quite meet his gaze. He told himself they were from exhaustion. Another part of him knew it was more.

"Nothing concerning you is ever an imposition, Chrissy."

She didn't respond before he left the room, closing the door behind him. His heavy footfalls in the hall and down the stairs held her attention. Instead of relief he'd come for Lucy, Christina felt bereft, a sense of loss she hadn't experienced since Millie's death.

It made no sense. She should be excited about her and Cici moving into their own house tomorrow, at the future the change would make. Chrissy knew many people felt she and Hex might have a future. She told herself single men didn't approach her because of it, even as she knew their lack of interest had no connection to the deputy. Christina simply didn't appeal to the eligible men in town.

At twenty-one, she had responsibility of her nine-year-old sister. Most men had no desire to saddle themselves with a wife and young girl. At least she hadn't met any. Not even Hex or Zeke had shown any interest beyond her help with Lucy.

Zeke might act as if he didn't care for any one woman, but it wasn't true. Since Francesca O'Reilly arrived on a stage with four other friends of Rachel Pelletier months before, he'd been smitten with the beautiful, auburn-haired lawyer. Chrissy feared if he didn't make his move soon, someone else would.

"Hex." She whispered his name while shirking out of her wrapper, tossing it on top of the coverlet. How she'd hoped he'd see her as more than a friend. Instead, he'd become fascinated with one of the new women in town.

Alana Hanrahan. Christina wanted to hate her, wanted to learn something horrible about the stunning beauty. She hadn't missed the way she and Hex looked at each other, the obvious interest. It had made her ill. It had also forced her to accept Hex would never be hers.

Slipping under the covers, she pulled them to her chin, closing her eyes. An image of Hex laughing pierced her heart, but she ruthlessly shoved it aside. The way she'd overcome the tragedies of her past assured Christina the feelings she held for Hex would diminish with time.

At some point, there would be someone who could love her and accept Cici. It just wouldn't be Hex Boudreaux.

Hawke DeBell fought the whipping winds and pounding rain from the latest Montana storm. It had started within an hour of leaving the territorial capital of Big Pine.

He'd been tracking his prey for weeks, following them across half the states. Those who recognized the two men from the tattered wanted posters he carried indicated they headed west toward Splendor.

Good news for the trail-weary bounty hunter. Two men he'd fought with during the war were deputies. They'd encouraged him to speak with the sheriff, Gabe Evans, about becoming a deputy. He didn't have a real interest, but sent a telegram agreeing to a meeting.

A mile out from Splendor, the storm tapered to a drizzle before the sky cleared. Reining to a stop, Hawke removed his duster, tying it behind the saddle before checking his sidearms and his rifle. Satisfied they were dry, he slid them away and swung into the saddle.

The people he tracked knew he followed. They might not know his identify, but Hawke had no doubt they were on the run.

The first buildings he spotted when entering Splendor were a large church and stately hotel, both appearing rather new compared to the shops he passed. At mid-afternoon on a Monday, the boardwalk and streets bustled with activity.

The size of the town surprised him. Most buildings were occupied, shoppers leaving stores with their arms laden with purchases. It wasn't the small frontier town he'd been led to believe.

According to a few who thought they recognized the outlaws, he was sure they'd changed their appearance. Hawke always seemed to be one step behind, a rare occurrence during his life as a bounty hunter.

Passing several women on his way to the jail, he tipped his hat. He hadn't been with a woman since leaving his wife and children to fight for the Southern cause, refusing to sully his wife's memory with someone he cared nothing about.

Still, his mother had taught him to be a gentleman. Even broken, he could do that much.

Reining up in front of the jail, he slid to the ground, taking a slow look around. Several people stared at him, their gazes blank. He'd come to expect the curiosity. Small towns everywhere were wary of strangers. Having no emotional ties to any of the locals, newcomers tended to be the ones to spark trouble and ride out.

Hawke wasn't that man. He'd take care of business and move on, shunning attachments for freedom.

Drawing the rifle from its scabbard, he stepped onto the boardwalk, hesitating a moment before going inside. Two deputies approached from different directions. As they drew closer, the corners of his mouth tipped upward, the closest he got to a full grin.

"Hawke DeBell. Damn, it's good to see you." Cash extended his hand, drawing him close for a hardy slap on the back. "It's been too long."

Beau did the same, stepping away to study his friend, seeing the deep lines on his face. "How have you been?"

"Can't complain."

Cash snorted a chuckle. "Come inside and meet the sheriff. We've got coffee. Not great, but it will wash down the trail dust."

Beau opened the jail door, motioning Hawke inside. Behind the desk, a broad-shouldered man studied wanted posters, lifting his head and standing at their approach.

"You must be Hawke DeBell. I'm Gabe Evans, the sheriff in Splendor." He extended his hand, gripping the one offered.

"Good to meet you, Sheriff."

"Have a seat."

"If you don't mind, I'll stand for a while. I've been on the trail since Big Pine."

"Not at all." Gabe moved to the stove, pouring coffee for Hawke while Cash and Beau took two of the chairs. Handing him the cup, Gabe sat back down. "What brought you this way?"

"I've been following two men since they robbed a series of banks back east." Digging into a pocket, he retrieved the ragged papers, handing them to Gabe. "Do you recognize them?"

Rubbing his chin, he studied the faces, at least what he could see of them wearing full beards and mustaches. "They look somewhat familiar, but I can't place them. Cash, Beau, have you seen these men?" He slid the wanted posters across the desk.

Cash stared at the images, shaking his head. "I wonder if they're two of the men involved in the shooting at the boardinghouse."

Beau's mouth twisted into a grimace. "You should show these to Hex and Zeke."

"All the deputies will see these. Are they wanted for anything other than the bank robberies?"

Hawke leaned against the wall, crossing his arms. "Suspected of robbing stages and one train. Personally, I don't think they robbed the train. There were five men involved. I haven't known them to ride with anyone but each other."

"You said they started back east?" Gabe asked.

"Virginia. Moved through North Carolina, Tennessee, Kentucky, and Missouri before riding through Iowa and into the Dakotas. They're known to hit small town banks and stages heading west. I believe they're headed to the Pacific, maybe San Francisco."

Shoving from the wall, Hawke grabbed a chair, swinging it around to straddle it. "I don't know where they're hiding the money. From what I can tell, they just keep riding, never stopping to bury or conceal what they've stolen. One of the people who saw this in Big Pine said the younger one no longer had a mustache or beard. Don't know if it's true, but I have to consider it. What's this about a shooting?"

Gabe rested his arms on the desk, clasping his hands together. "Three men wearing handkerchiefs shot a diner at the boardinghouse restaurant. He was at a table with four others. None of them recognized anything about the shooters and said they'd just met the dead man that evening."

"Shooters got away?" Hawke asked.

"Yes. Two of my deputies were in the restaurant. They had a woman friend and two young girls with them. It happened so fast, they had no time to react, and didn't want to leave the girls alone. I'm good with their decision. They questioned the diners, learned the four came in on the stage from Cheyenne on Saturday. I don't believe there's a connection between the shooting and the men you're tracking, but you're welcome to talk to the people who were at the table."

Hawke rubbed his stubbled jaw, mouth tight in concentration. "I don't see a connection, either."

"Are you determined to continue until you find the two men?" Gabe wanted to talk about the town's need for another deputy. Two to three more, but right now, he'd be happy with one.

"Haven't decided." Pressing his palms against his eyes, Hawke fought the exhaustion from too many days on the trail, a diet of hardtack and jerky, and too little sleep. "I may stay around here for a while."

Cash grinned at Beau. "Long enough to meet our wives, share several meals, and let us show you around. I think you'll be surprised at the size of Splendor. There are a good number of successful ranches and farms."

"Including the largest spread in the territory," Beau added.

Hawke's eyes flashed in interest, but he didn't comment. Standing, he swung the chair around, placing it next to the desk.

"Do you need a place to stay?"

He gave a slow nod at Gabe. "The boardinghouse will be fine."

"Suzanne has clean rooms and excellent food. Beau and I will walk over with you." Cash shoved to his feet. "We'll be joining you for supper." He left no room for Hawke to argue.

Rising, Gabe stuck out his hand. "Good to meet you. Let's plan on talking again tomorrow." With a nod, he and the deputies left.

Gabe walked to the window, watching as they crossed the street to Suzanne's. He admired Hawke, his tenacity at tracking the robbers across the country. The man was driven. To succeed at bringing in the robbers or to put the past behind him, Gabe didn't know.

What he did know was he wanted Hawke to stay in Splendor.

Chapter Nine

Christina brushed a hand across her forehead before shoving the empty trunk into the closet in her bedroom. *Her* bedroom. It had been over a year since she hadn't shared a bed with one of her sisters.

Cici couldn't be more excited. Although not nearly as opulent as her bedroom in Kansas City, she loved having her own space, privacy unavailable at the boardinghouse. The best part—it wasn't far from where Lucy lived.

"What now, Chrissy?" Cici stood with her hands clasped before her, watching as the trunk disappeared into the closet.

"What can I do?" Lucy jumped up and down, clapping her hands.

Christina had brought them straight from school to the house, their excitement confirming she'd made the right decision. The tension she'd been feeling dissolved the longer they were in the cozy home.

The move the day before had been uneventful. Noah brought a wagon, helped Hex and Zeke load their belongings, and stayed to carry trunks and their few pieces of furniture inside. She'd made him promise to bring Abby and their son, Gabriel, over for supper the following week.

After shooing Hex and Zeke out, Christina and the girls got to work. They made a game of putting away enough of their belongings to feel comfortable the first night. Even though a school night, Lucy would be staying with Cici.

"That's all for now. We need to get supper started."

Zeke and Hex had talked her into bringing the girls to their place to make supper instead of hauling pots of stew or roast between the houses. At first, she'd hesitated, wanting to limit her time around Hex.

Thinking about it after the men had left on Sunday, she grudgingly let go of her stubbornness. Making supper at their place would be much easier, plus she could bring a smaller portion of supper back to her house.

"Get your coats and we'll go." A rap on the door had her rushing through the living room to pull it open. "Hex. What are you doing here?"

Mouth quirking into a slight grin, he removed his hat. "I wanted to see how you're doing, and check on Lucy."

Hearing her father's voice, she ran toward him. "Papa!" Falling into his open arms, Lucy hugged him, then jumped back. "Isn't the house nice?"

He didn't ruin her mood by saying it was the same layout as their home. All the houses on the street had been built by Noah and his workers. Some had one bedroom, most had two, and a few had three. He and Zeke rented the largest so they'd each have their own bedroom.

It had been an extravagance they couldn't afford, but both had wanted Lucy to have her own place in a home with two men. Many mornings, he awoke with Lucy in his bed. She'd lost so much in her young life, he didn't have the heart to insist she stay in her own room. Doc Worthington said she'd grow out of it in time, warning Hex not to make too much of it.

"Yes, the house is quite nice." He continued to stand on the porch, waiting for an invitation inside.

"Sorry. Please, come in." Christina stepped aside, taking a more critical look around the room. One chair, a small table with a kerosene lamp, and an old rug which had belonged to her father. It had been in his study, a present from his first wife. Her mother.

Hex circled the room, turning toward her. "Noah keeps extra furniture in a room behind the livery. You might ask him if you can take a look."

"He mentioned it. I've ordered furniture to be shipped here from the house in Kansas City. I'll use some and place the rest in Noah's storage cabin."

Hex understood. "Seems you have everything decided." For the first time, he noticed they all wore coats. "Are you leaving?"

Christina felt her face flush. "I considered what you said, and decided it would be best to cook supper at your house. If you don't mind, I'll bring some back here for Cici and me."

Hex concealed his surprise. "I'd rather you stay and have supper with us."

She thought of Alana, the way he'd looked at her, deferred to the beautiful woman. "We should return here. I've a lot more work to do. Perhaps another time."

Letting out a disappointed breath, Hex nodded. "If you're sure. I'll escort you three beautiful ladies back to my place."

Christina hesitated a moment before turning away to get her reticule while the girls giggled at his playful tone. Hex was so good with the girls. The same with Zeke. They treated Cici the same as Lucy, which made limiting their time with the men hard. They were excellent role models, kind, and protective.

Taking an empty pot from a cupboard, Christina met them at the door. Reaching out, Hex took it from her hand, closing the door behind them.

"Miss Murton says the town is having a party. Is it true, Papa?" Lucy took her father's hand, smiling as she looked up at him.

He glanced at Christina before answering. "I believe they're calling it a celebration."

"Will it have clowns and games?" Her excited voice had the adults smiling.

"Maybe. I'm not sure about all the town has planned. There will be competition between the cowboys and shooting contests."

"What about games?" Lucy persisted.

Christina responded first. "I heard from Suzanne the church women are planning games and having a bake sale."

"Will you be making something?" Cici asked, slowing her pace when a woman she recognized as a friend of Zeke's approached them.

"Good afternoon, Hex, Chrissy." Francesca O'Reilly, green eyes flashing in welcome, braided auburn hair tossed over her shoulder, smiled at the small group.

Hex acknowledged her with a grin. "Hello, Francesca. You know Christina and Cecilia McKenna."

"Of course." She didn't say how much the four looked like a real family, or that she knew Christina helped the Boudreaux brothers with Lucy. "How is everyone?"

"Good. Chrissy and Cici moved into the house next to Isabella and Travis."

Francesca switched her attention to Christina. "Is that right? I've been talking to Noah about renting one of the vacant houses."

"There are several vacant ones between me and the clinic. We've only been there one night, but it's very quiet."

Francesca chuckled. "My room at the boardinghouse is wonderful, but the noise..." She lifted a brow, giving a slight shrug.

"I know. Plus the dust of being on the main street. You should ask Noah about the one next to us. It's got one bedroom, unless you need a bigger place."

"No. One bedroom is perfect. I should let you go."

"Have supper with us tonight, Frannie." Hex offered the invitation without thought. His brother had been smitten with her since she and four of her friends traveled to Splendor from New York. Hex was trying to give Zeke a little push before he lost her to one of the growing number of single men in town.

"I don't want to be a bother."

"You won't be," Chrissy assured her. If Francesca came over, perhaps she and Cici would stay, also. "And there's always plenty."

Hex rested a hand on Lucy's shoulder. "Besides, Zeke is planning to have supper with us before heading to the jail."

Christina had never seen Francesca blush, but she did now. "You don't think he'd mind me being there?"

Hex gave a brief shake of his head. "He might be surprised, but he'll welcome your presence, Frannie. As will the rest of us. Right, Chrissy?"

She winced, realizing his intention. He'd easily put her in a position where she and Cici would have to stay or appear inhospitable. Clearing her throat, she nodded.

"Yes. It would be nice having another woman at the table."

"I do have some work to finish at the office. What time should I be there?" As one of two attorneys in town, and the only woman, she'd struggled at first for clients. Over the months, Francesca had been able to draw enough clients to pay the bills.

"Zeke will be home at five," Hex offered.

"I'll be there. Thank you again for the invitation." She gave a quick wave of her hand, turning to return to her office.

Christina gave him a strained glance as they continued to his house. "I hope Zeke doesn't decide to eat at the boardinghouse."

"I'll make certain he doesn't." He handed her the small pot. "I need to go by the jail and look for Zeke. Are you all right getting the girls back to my place?"

Snorting, Christina shot him a glance, leaving no doubt as to how foolish the question was.

Hex stopped, rubbing the back of his neck. "Never mind. I'll see you all later."

"Bye, Papa."

Turning to see Lucy give him a wave, he lifted his hand in return, a smile curving his lips. What had once seemed an insurmountable burden had become the best thing that had ever happened in his life.

Slipping between the buildings toward the main street, he took his time walking along the boardwalk toward the jail. Plenty could still happen in the rough cow town before it was time to go home.

A few buildings before reaching the jail, he spotted a tall, wiry man with golden-brown skin and auburn hair slide from his saddle. Removing his hat, he made a slow turn, exposing long hair tied with a leather thong at the nape of his neck.

Hex wondered at his reason for being in Splendor. With the pair of ivory handled six-shooters strapped around his hips, he doubted the man made a living moving cattle.

Flattening his back to the side of the building, Hex continued to watch, readying to approach the stranger when the man stepped onto the boardwalk and walked toward the jail. Taking one more look around, he opened the door and stepped inside.

Unable to ignore his curiosity, Hex followed, slowing to study the beautiful Palomino Pinto stallion belonging to the newcomer. Letting out a low whistle at the stunning animal, he continued to the jail.

He could hear Gabe's voice through the door, assuming the second one belonged to the stranger. Stepping inside, he hung his hat on a hook before leaning against the nearest wall.

Gabe continued talking about Splendor as if he hadn't entered. After a couple minutes, Hex realized the man sitting across the desk from the sheriff was a new deputy.

"Hex, meet Shane Banderas. He's just hired on as a deputy."

Extending his hand, he clasped Shane's. "You've got a beautiful stallion."

"I've had him since a pony. He's saved my life more than once."

"Sit down and join us, Hex." Gabe motioned to a chair. "Shane rode in a few weeks ago, but had to head down to Wyoming to deliver a prisoner north to the prison near Deer Lodge."

"You're a U.S. Marshal?" Hex asked.

"Deputy in Cheyenne. Our marshal and a prisoner were killed by Shoshone. The Army sent out a patrol, but never found their tracks. The sheriff thought I might have better luck moving a different prisoner through Wyoming to Montana."

"Did you?" Hex relaxed, enjoying the story.

"I'm here, aren't I?" He didn't smile when he answered, shifting his attention to Gabe. "Where do the other deputies live?"

"A few are married and have places in and outside of town. The rest live in houses on the streets behind the jail. Noah Brandt built them and rents them at a good price to my men. I'll talk to him for you. The last I knew, there's a one bedroom place next to the woman who helps take care of Hex's daughter. She just moved in yesterday."

Startled by his boss's comment, Hex sat mute for long moments, thinking about the good-looking deputy moving next door to Chrissy. He didn't need competition for her attention, especially with her thinking he held an interest in Alana.

Hex thought of the beautiful woman who'd ridden into town in the back of a covered wagon. He knew she found him attractive. When he tried to envision a future with her, the image wouldn't come. They hadn't been around each other enough to make that happen.

He could take the time to get to know Alana better. His mind told him if he did, Christina would be lost to him. She was already putting distance between them. Her smiles had been limited to those involving the girls, their easy comradery gone after she'd seen him with Alana at McCall's.

Hex wondered if he'd feel the same if he encountered Christina out to supper with Shane. The tightening in his stomach assured him he would.

"Hex, did you hear me?"

His head shot up, having missed what Gabe had asked. "What did you say?"

"Why don't you take Shane to see the house next to Chrissy's? I'll talk to Noah and meet you there." Gabe stood, grabbing his hat. Reaching out, he clasped Shane's hand. "Glad to have you with us. I believe you're going to find Splendor to be a place you can call home."

For the second time in less than ten minutes, Hex's stomach clenched.

Chapter Ten

"Where are you going, Finn?" Alana moved next to him, noticing the somewhat clean clothes and hat he wore for special occasions. On normal nights, he'd be bunking down about now.

Strapping on his gunbelt, he turned to include everyone in his response. "The town is having a meeting about some kind of celebration. I want to be sure we don't miss out on anything."

"I'll go with you." Before Alana could move, he grabbed her arm.

"I'm going alone." He met her fuming gaze. "Do *not* follow me." Finn sent the same hard look at the others. "None of you. I'll let you know what I learn."

"Are we still opening the saloon tomorrow?" A slight, older man with graying stubble and ruddy complexion barely lifted his head from where he sat on a downed log.

"Yes. We'll work out problems as we go. Everyone has the same jobs as with the last three saloons. If we're lucky, we'll have enough to head out within a few months." Slipping into his coat with the least holes, he spoke to Brenda. "Attend to Dara while I'm gone."

"I will, Finn." Less flighty or vain than Alana, Brenda could be depended upon to take care of his wife.

Gripping the reins to his horse, he swung into the saddle, taking the trail to Splendor. His thoughts were split between the meeting tonight and what his family needed to accomplish in the next few months.

Their pattern had been set years ago and it couldn't be abandoned now. They made too much money, even if sneaking away in the middle of the night left no doors open for a return. Nothing was left behind, except perhaps a few broken hearts. Alana was a master at leading men on, getting them to empty their pockets at the saloon, then moving to the next man she fancied. Not one had caught her heart.

Splendor appeared to be different. Alana spoke about one of the deputies in a tone Finn had never heard and didn't like. Her interest in the man couldn't be mistaken.

Taking the last turn, he couldn't miss the extra lights coming from inside the community center building located behind the church. Nor could he ignore the number of wagons and horses outside. It seemed everyone in the area wanted to hear the latest on the first town celebration.

Finn had heard other town business would be discussed. He cared little about anything other than the festival and how the Hanrahans could benefit from it.

Entering the building, he took a seat at the back, recognizing the voice of Horace Clausen, president of Splendor Bank.

"Unless there are additional points we need to discuss, I'm calling for a vote to name our main street. Thank you to everyone who submitted a name, to those who took the time to vote." Horace fiddled with the tattered paper before him, smoothing it open on the lectern. "Even though it was the unofficial name since Splendor was founded, Main Street received few votes." He chuckled, as did several people in the audience.

"I won't delay the announcement any longer. By a vote of the people, from now on, our main street will be changed to Frontier Street."

A roar of applause, whoops, and cheers erupted, dying down when Horace held up his hand. "The street behind Frontier will change to Palace Street. The following street, named after the first man to offer medical services in Splendor, will be Worthington." He stopped again when everyone turned their attention to Charles Worthington, sitting in the audience with his recent bride, Clare. Shouts of approval and congratulations were exchanged. "The following street, where several of our deputies live, will be Rimrock, and the street down the center of Chinatown has been changed to Grant."

Releasing a slow breath, he folded the paper, slipping it into his coat pocket. "This was all decided by a vote of the townsfolk. There will be more decisions to make as the town grows. The next order of business is the community celebration. I'll turn this part over to Dax Pelletier."

Finn could feel excitement ripple through the crowd as the rancher stepped to the podium. "I'll make this short. Right after church a week from this Sunday, we'll be having a ranch rodeo, shooting competition, and other events for youngsters and adults." He glanced at his brother, Luke, before continuing. "We originally planned to have it close to town, but we don't have the corrals and pens necessary for the events we plan. Instead, it's going to be held at Redemption's Edge. For those of you new to Splendor, it's the ranch I own with my brother, Luke. We rode out to Fort Connall to talk with Colonel Miles McArthur. He and some of his men will be joining us. That's the reason we're pushing it off a week and moving it to a Sunday." Dax motioned for Luke to join him.

"For you who don't know me, I'm Luke Pelletier. This is what is planned."

He went through the events and shooting contests, number of contestants, and where to complete the registration. "We'll be preparing food for whoever shows up. The church women will be having a bake sale, so expect to spend some money." A broad smile crossed his face at the laughter from the audience. "The women will also set up games for the children. Anyone who wants to help out or get a form to participate can talk to me or Bull Mason." Luke nodded at one of their two foremen who sat with his wife, Lydia, near the front. "Any questions?"

The brothers fielded several questions before turning the meeting back to Horace. "Any of you business owners who want to set up a table to sell your wares, just let me know. If the celebration is successful, we'll start work on building corrals and pens so the next year's event can be held near town. One more announcement. Gabe, would you come on up?"

Taking a place by the podium, he made a brief announcement. "I've hired two additional deputies. Hawke DeBell and Shane Banderas, please stand. These men are joining the others who protect Splendor. They'll be making the rounds and introducing themselves." Heads bobbed while others clapped as Gabe sat down.

Horace returned to close the meeting. "Thank you all for coming by tonight. Hope to see you at Redemption's Edge."

Finn stood, hurrying toward Luke, along with several other business owners. Introducing himself, he asked about having a table with beer and spirits. As long as Finn didn't mind the Dixie having a table, he was assured it wouldn't be a problem.

The ride back to camp took longer in the total darkness. He occupied the time considering what he'd learned at the meeting. The rodeo would be a good place to let people know Finn's was open, the types of games offered, and other entertainment available. The last would be discussed quietly, being careful not to let the good church women know. They'd opened in other towns, closing down a lucrative part of the business when the married women learned of what went on in the rooms upstairs. He didn't want that to happen in Splendor.

Which meant Finn would have to find a way to keep Alana quiet. She had a tendency to speak when she shouldn't, and in this case, her infatuation with the deputy could cause a problem.

Not that the sheriff would close them down. Ruby's Palace offered entertainment on the stage downstairs, plus a different kind in the rooms on the second floor. Even so, other than drinking and games, Finn preferred to keep the rest quiet.

If it took sabotaging her connection to the deputy, he had no problem protecting the family by making that happen.

"Deputy Boudreaux!" Hex slowed and cringed, turning slowly toward the singsong voice he recognized. Alana came toward him on the boardwalk, a sultry grin matched the sway of her hips. His chest tightened a tiny bit, acknowledging her beauty. At least outside. He wasn't sure about inside. Tipping his hat, he waited for her to stop beside him.

"Miss Hanrahan. How are you this morning?"

"Very well, thank you. Did you know we are opening Finn's at noon today?"

"Yes, I'd heard."

She ran fingers down his sleeve, fiddling with the hem a moment before dropping her hand. Her lips curled, a twinkle in her eyes. "I could buy you the first beer."

"A nice offer. Unfortunately, I'm working and have plans for the rest of the day."

Alana blinked, unprepared to be turned down. Shoving aside the disappointment, she forced a grin. "Well, I'll be working this evening. Surely you have a few minutes to stop by."

He held back a chuckle. Alana's forward behavior could be endearing. Today, he found it annoying. "I'm afraid I must decline. Did you hear about the celebration and rodeo out at the Pelletier ranch?"

The change of subject confused her. "The Pelletiers?"

"They're the largest landowners in Montana. Run cattle and breed horses for the Army. The ranch rodeo will be at their place, along with shooting contests, food, drink, and games for the children."

He didn't miss the way her nose curled on the last. "How lovely."

"It's a week from Sunday. Perhaps your family would be interested in attending."

"Can't I ride with you, Deputy Boudreaux? It would be a much more pleasant experience." Again, she touched his arm, showing no reaction when he stepped away.

"I'll be sorry to miss the ride with you. This trip, my wagon is full with my daughter, her best friend, Miss

McKenna, Miss O'Reilly, and my brother, Zeke. He's also a deputy."

Her face fell a little with each name. Glancing over his shoulder, she spotted the woman who took care of his daughter and cleaned. Seeing the woman watching her, she moved closer to Hex, came up on tiptoes and brushed a kiss across his cheek.

His eyes narrowed on her, mouth twisting in displeasure. "What are you doing, Alana?" Hex tried to be subtle about swiping his hand over the spot.

"Don't you like it?"

Not wanting to be rude, he didn't respond, taking another step away. "I should get back on my rounds, Alana. Best of luck on the opening of your saloon." Turning, he crossed the street, coming up short when he saw Christina standing on the boardwalk, watching. He made a quick decision to draw attention away from what she saw. Taking her hand, he slipped her arm through his, walking in the opposite direction.

"Good morning, Chrissy."

"Good morning, Hex. Wasn't that Alana?" She glanced back over her shoulder, trying to pull her arm free. The effort caused him to tighten his hold.

"Yes."

"She's quite free with her attentions, isn't she?"

Hex looked down at her, glad to see the spark in her eyes and slow grin spreading across her face. "Yes, she is." He chuckled, thinking of how she kissed him this morning. "Alana is more forward than any woman I've met in a long time."

"You don't like it?"

He stopped, turning her to face him. "*Not* from her, Chrissy." Before she could reply, he continued along the boardwalk.

"Did you know Gabe hired two deputies this week?"

She blinked, mind still spinning from his comment. "Uh...no. Who are they?"

"Hawke De Bell and Shane Banderas. They may be in the jail if you'd like to meet them."

Eyes wide, she shook her head. "Another time. I still must go to the meat market, the vegetable shop in Chinatown, and bakery. Is it all right to put flour, sugar, molasses, and salt on your account at the general store?"

Squeezing her hand, he leaned down, lowering his voice. "Chrissy, you can put whatever you need on the account. Zeke and I are out of soap to clean up. And get the girls a peppermint stick apiece."

"All right." She swallowed the knot of confusion building in her stomach.

Hex had never strolled with her as if they were a couple. His hard body brushing against hers created strange feelings, her breath catching at the contact. She didn't look forward to when he'd have to let her go. "The general store is right here."

Stopping, he didn't disengage her arm from his. "Would you be free to join me for lunch?"

A brow lifted. "Lunch?"

"Yes. Unless you have other plans." Again, he squeezed her hand.

The look on his face showed a faint amount of vulnerability, something she'd never associated with Hex. Strong, confident, and prone to take charge of any situation, his request confused her.

Wasn't he interested in Alana? Then she thought of his quick response to her question about the woman's rather bold behavior.

"Lunch would be lovely, Hex. Where shall I meet you?"

"Do you mind going to McCall's?"

She thought of last week when she'd met Josie. Hex and Alana were a few tables away, oblivious to anyone else in the restaurant. With only three eating places in Splendor, one of them more expensive, there wasn't much of a choice.

"Not at all. I love Betts's cooking."

A slow breath of relief blew through his lips. "Noon?"

"Perfect. I'll see you then." Hurrying into the general store, she stopped several steps inside, placing a hand to her chest. She could feel her heart pound against her ribs, stomach fluttering with anticipation.

"It's only lunch with a friend," she whispered to herself, feeling silly. "He isn't courting you. He's simply being nice."

Then why did it feel like so much more?

Chapter Eleven

"We can't stay in town any longer, Ma. At some point, they're going to tie Pa and me to the robberies."

Ma Groom sent a warning look at her son, then to her adopted daughter. They'd been complaining for days about the delay in leaving Splendor.

"Pa says it's safer for us to go along with what the sheriff wants. He hopes to catch the men who shot Steed and wants us here for the trial. Right now, he and the deputies believe we're four people traveling together to San Francisco. If we slip away, he'll send men after us, maybe notify the law between here and the Pacific."

Junior shredded a shaky hand through his short hair. He missed the longer tresses his folks had insisted he cut when they changed their look several towns back.

The four had told the sheriff and his deputies they'd arrived on the stage from Cheyenne instead of coming from the east through Big Pine. They'd changed their look slightly with each robbery after entering the Dakotas until shaving their beards, cleaning up, and donning the clothes of city businessmen and society women. The changes had kept the bounty hunter days behind them. If only they knew his identity.

Their elaborate ruse had worked better than expected. The women traveled by stage while Pa Groom and Junior stayed on horseback, joining Ma Groom and Sissy when it suited their purpose. While the men planned each robbery, the women made friends with locals, keeping in touch with them as they moved from town to town. It was how they'd learned about the bounty hunter. As far as they knew, he hadn't followed them to Splendor. At least not yet.

"The longer we stay, the bigger the risk the bounty hunter will show up here, Ma."

"He'll be looking for two outlaws, not four city folk traveling by stage to San Francisco."

"Ma's right, Junior." Sissy sat on the bed in the room she shared with her brother.

He rounded on her, fists clenched at his sides. "You know nothing about what goes on in this family."

"Junior," his mother warned, but he ignored her.

"She's not a *real* part of our family."

"Sissy is as much a sister as if she were blood."

Junior barked out a mirthless laugh, his gaze moving between the two women. "If she were blood, we wouldn't be sleeping in the same bed." Hearing a gasp from Sissy, his anger began to wane. "I'm sorry. I shouldn't have said that."

Visibly shaken, Sissy stood, walking to the window. "It's the truth. You've been taking what you want from me for a long time." She wouldn't admit the obvious. Sissy loved Junior, carried his child, although she hadn't shared the news of her pregnancy with anyone.

He walked to her, placing a hand on Sissy's shoulder. "You know I care about you."

She stepped away, his hand dropping to his side. "But you don't love or even like me."

Shaking his head, Junior swallowed the pain of what she believed. "I like you fine."

Didn't she understand he had to think of her as not a real part of his family? They'd been sleeping together since he'd turned seventeen and she was fifteen. He loved her, but it wouldn't be wise to let her or his parents know the extent of his caring. Junior knew in his heart his parents would send one of them away, and he couldn't bear the thought of being without her. They'd run away before that happened. He had to return to his original concern.

"Something isn't right, Ma. I can feel it right here." His fist touched his chest.

"Then you'd best talk to Pa. He makes the decisions."

Junior knew it would do no good to speak to the elder Groom. Once his mind was made up, there was no changing it. He thought of the money stashed away for his and Sissy's eventual escape. Money his Pa knew nothing about. Money he and Sissy may need much sooner than expected.

Hex sipped his coffee, watching Christina eat the last bite of the generous portion of meatloaf Betts had served up. Lifting her head, a smile curved her lips, hitting him as hard as a blow to his gut. Her smiles always impacted him this way.

The same as Lucy, Christina brought sunshine into a life darkened by too much tragedy. Hex knew he could count on Zeke when their family was threatened, but it was Christina who provided a sense of peace, of sanity in a world filled with grim reality and difficult choices.

He couldn't believe he'd entertained the idea Alana could hold a place in his life. After their last encounter, Hex didn't know if he even liked the woman. Some good came from the encounters with the newcomer.

After months of denying it, Hex accepted his feelings for Christina ran deep. Holding out his cup when Betts came by with a pot of coffee, he thanked her, then turned his attention back to the woman across the table.

"I'd like some of Betts's apple pie. How about you?"

Pressing the napkin to her mouth, she shook her head. "I couldn't possibly eat another bite. Don't let it stop you from having dessert." The pleasant sensation of being with Hex dissipated at the sight of Alana looking inside the restaurant. A moment later, the bell over the door chimed.

"Why, Deputy Boudreaux, what a nice surprise. May I join you?"

Alana's voice caused a sick feeling to form in his stomach. Standing, he shook his head. "Unfortunately, Miss McKenna and I are ready to leave." Glancing at Christina, he didn't miss the tense lines on her face relax. "Perhaps another time." It was a pleasantry, one he had no plans of fulfilling.

Forgetting about the pie, he dug money from his pocket, placing it on the table before helping Christina up. Settling a hand on her elbow, Hex started for the door.

"Wait." Alana touched his arm, her mouth drawing into a pout. "Will you be coming to the saloon tonight?"

Feeling Chrissy stiffen next to him, Hex shook his head. "I already have plans for supper at home with my family." He thought of supper the night when Francesca had joined them. The stunned expression on Zeke's face at seeing her in the house had quickly been replaced with delight.

Alana's gaze narrowed on Christina, her displeasure clear. "Perhaps someday I'll be included in your group of friends."

Hex didn't answer before opening the door to escort Chrissy outside. Slipping her arm through his, he kept a hand over hers, wishing the end of their meal had been as exceptional as the rest of it.

"I'm not interested in Alana, Chrissy."

The comment stunned her, catching her unguarded. "I thought, well…"

Tightening his hold, he looked down at her. "I have no desire to spend time with her. It's important you understand that."

Her mind whirled with possible reasons he no longer held an interest in Alana. Was he simply being a friend, sharing his thoughts? Could he be warning her to stay away from Alana? Might the unthinkable be happening, and Hex was considering courting her?

The last had her swallowing...hard. She so wanted it to be the last, but refused to allow herself to hope. Thinking back on the last year, he'd never given any indication he had feelings beyond friendship. A strong friendship, yes. Did he desire her, want to spend his life with her? It was absurd to even consider it.

"All right."

"I'd appreciate it if you'd keep her away from the girls. Alana doesn't need to know about them."

Ah. His concern was all about Lucy and Cici.

Her throat tightened in disappointment. "Of course. There's rarely a time the three of us walk on the main, I mean, Frontier Street. Unless I have to stop for something, we go from school, past the livery, and down Rimrock Street to your house, or to mine." She chanced a look at him, trying to force even a weak smile, unable to manage it.

"I knew I could depend on you, Chrissy. Shall I walk you back to the house?"

"No need. There's still time to get my shopping done before meeting the girls at school. Thank you for lunch." Slipping her arm from his, she watched Alana cross to the other side of the street, displeased at Hex's rejection. "I'll see you at your place."

"You and Cici will be staying tonight for supper."

"Is that an invitation, Deputy Boudreaux?"

Her flirty tone had the corners of his mouth twitching, brow lifting "Yes, it is, Miss McKenna."

"Then we'll be quite pleased to join you." With a slight wave, she left him on the boardwalk, his mouth agape.

He'd never seen this playful side of Christina and it intrigued him. The sudden sway of her hips held his interest until she stepped to the door of the general store. Stopping long enough to glance back at him and wave again, she disappeared inside.

Settling fisted hands on his hips, he looked down at the wood slats beneath his boots and shook his head. How had he been so blind? His friends were right. Christina had definitely crossed the line to become a beautiful, desirable woman.

Hawke sat next to Shane, the two new deputies comparing their experiences in hushed tones as they scanned Frontier Street. Not much had happened all day, except for spotting the young man sitting on a bench outside the St. James.

Hawke motioned with his hand. "You ever seen the man in the suit across the street?"

Shane switched his attention to a younger man with short hair, dark pants, coat, and hat. He fidgeted with the lapel of his coat, gaze darting around as if he couldn't find a suitable place to focus.

"Never seen him. Why?"

"He looks like one of the two people I've been following across the country. Cleaned up, but there's still similarities." Hawke pulled out the wanted posters, handing them to Shane, who studied them before returning them.

"There may be a slight resemblance, but..." Shane's mouth twisted into a smirk. "Did your man start out as a dandy?" He referred to the clothes the man wore today.

"I don't know what the men did back east. Probably small time outlaws, breaking into businesses, and robbing those weaker than them. Those kind always prey on the weak and vulnerable." Hawke massaged the back of his neck. "They're probably all the way to the Pacific by now."

"Better there in that rowdy, lawless town than here." Shane shot one more glance at the young man, seeing his hands twitch in his lap. "Sure is a nervous sort."

"Who's a nervous sort?" Hex leaned against the wall beside them, following Shane's gaze.

"The man sitting outside the St. James. Do you know him?" Hawke couldn't let go of the possibility he'd seen the man before.

"He's one of the three men who were at a table in the boardinghouse restaurant with two women, one older and one younger. One of the three men was shot by gunmen who entered the restaurant. The other

111

surviving man is older than the one sitting across the street. Why?"

Hawke's lips pressed together. "Something about him reminds me of the younger of the two outlaws I've been tracking."

"Talk to him at the jail. Use the shooting as the reason."

Hawke gave a slow shake of his head. "Not yet. How much longer do you think the four will stay in town?"

Hex's brow lifted, shrugging. "Gabe hasn't given his approval for them to leave. Doesn't mean they won't take off anyway. He's got no reason to keep them here. Gabe told them they'd be safer in Splendor until we found the men who gun downed their friend. Hell, all of us believe those men have vanished from the territory. I think he believes the four were somehow involved in the man's death. Maybe know the three who shot him."

Scratching his jaw, Hawke took one more careful glance at the man on the bench. He'd stopped fidgeting, staring down at the hands clasped in his lap.

"I'm going to keep watch on him. What I need is to see him with his older companion. Maybe when the two are together, I'll be able to make a decision about talking to them."

"They eat at McCall's or the boardinghouse most days." Hex pushed away from the wall. "I wouldn't wait long. Gabe's warning won't hold them here much longer."

Chapter Twelve

Jerome Taggert paced their camp a couple miles from Splendor, muttering to himself as he came to a decision. They'd done their part in eliminating a threat and hadn't been paid. That was about to change. Stopping, he stared at his twin brothers, Theo and Byron.

"I'm riding to town tonight. You two stay here. Be ready to ride when I return."

Four years younger than Jerome, his brothers had been his constant shadows since they were five. When he was thirteen, their father had taken off with a woman he met at the local saloon, forcing Jerome to quit school. He'd worked alongside his mother to keep the ranch going. Although they made small payments, it hadn't been enough.

Another year passed before the bank could no longer extend their loan. It hadn't been what the manager wanted, but the bank's board made the final decision. He'd stretched out the eviction as long as he could. Still, losing the ranch had been a hard blow to the family. Their mother in particular.

They'd moved to live with her sister, a spinster who loved her sister, but had little use for children. The three boys did what they could to help around the house, including taking care of one cow, three head of cattle, an older horse, several chickens, a few pigs, and the large garden. Their mother cleaned the house, leaving little for their aunt to do except eat, sleep, and watch them work. In exchange, they had a home.

They fell into a routine, the boys returning to school for a few years before tragedy struck. Their mother became ill, succumbing to the cancer ravaging her body. Her death changed everything.

"We should go with you, Jerome." Theo walked toward his horse, planning to saddle it. Byron stood, meaning to follow.

"No. They'll be looking for three men." He checked the guns strapped around his hips. "I plan to find the man who hired us, get what's owed, and ride out."

If the man balked, he'd use his skills at persuasion to change his mind. Afterward, he and his brothers would disappear.

Byron moved to stop Jerome's path to the horses. "At least let one of us go. I don't have a good feeling about you going alone."

"I'm not leaving just one of you behind. I won't be gone long. Be packed and ready to leave when I get back." He clasped both brothers on their shoulders as he passed them. "Keep watch and don't sleep. We aren't that far off the main trail and anyone could see the fire." He continued to his horse and grabbed the reins, swinging into the saddle.

Theo shot a look at Byron, communicating without saying a word.

"Stay close to camp." Taking a concealed path to the main trail, he lifted his hand in a wave.

The twins waited five minutes before stomping out the fire, saddling their own horses, and following. They'd always faced life as a team. The three Taggert brothers against the world. As long as they stayed together, everything worked out fine. Which meant they weren't going to let Jerome face any possible threat alone.

Christina took the bowl from Hex's hand, drying it before setting it inside the cupboard. Supper had been perfect. Zeke helped with the meal, deciding he'd prefer the company of his family over strangers in the boardinghouse. She'd laughed at his remark. Anyone who met Zeke soon understood his initial friendliness didn't guarantee a friendship. He'd left shortly after supper, leaving her and Hex with the two girls.

"That's the last." Hex dried his hands, leaning his muscular body against the edge of the counter. "I'm glad you and Cici stayed. Supper is always better with the two of you here."

She flashed him a cautious smile, wiping her hands down her apron before removing it. Christina wanted to believe he preferred her company to the other single women in town. Most notably Alana.

Inexperience and lack of confidence when it came to men had her dismissing his comments. Although she hadn't gotten along with her late stepmother, Mirna, at least one of the woman's observations made sense.

"Don't ever trust what men say, Christina. They lie as easily as they drink whiskey."

She had scoffed at the warning, knowing Mirna's own tendency to lie. Over time, she'd matured, accepting her father had cheated on their mother, committed adultery as if his actions didn't affect anyone else. She'd come to love and hate him the years after their mother's death, a sense of ambivalence wrapping around her as they lowered his coffin into the ground.

So yes, Mirna's counsel, unwanted as it was, weighed on her. Before today and his invitation to lunch, Hex had never shown an interest in her the same as with Alana. She suspected his actions today had more to do with his concerns of losing her as a helper than any caring.

"Supper *was* nice, Hex." Hanging the apron on a hook, she went to gather Cici. "We should go before it gets any later."

Continuing to lean against the counter, he watched as she stepped outside, calling her younger sister. It bothered him how different Christina had been since the incident in McCall's. He no longer believed the chill between them had to do with Alana's comment. Every instinct told him it was something else. Waiting until she and the girls walked back inside, he shoved away from the counter.

"Are you going to be able to get Lucy tomorrow?"

Brows drawing together, Christina studied his face, confused by the question. "I get them every day, Hex. Why do you ask?"

Slipping his thumbs into the waistband of his jeans, he took a couple steps toward her. "I want to make sure I'm not taking advantage."

Her gaze moved over his features as her mind worked to understand what was behind the question. Not once had he doubted her desire to help with his daughter. Why now? The only answer she could imagine was he'd found someone else to take care of Lucy.

"You aren't taking advantage of me. I enjoy being with the girls after school. Would you rather ask someone else?" She held her breath, praying he'd say no. Instead, he didn't answer the question.

"What about cooking supper and cleaning? Those are beyond what we talked about in the beginning."

Christina rocked back on her heels, wishing he had answered her question before asking one of his own. "I don't mind." Her voice was so low he had to step closer.

"What?"

Lifting her head, she jutted her chin toward him. "I don't mind the work, Hex. But if you've got someone else you want watching her, I'll understand."

Moving until he stood inches away, he raised his hand, stroking his fingers down the soft skin of her cheek. "Do you want to tell me what's bothering you?"

She leaned into his hand before comprehending her reaction to his touch. Straightening, she took a step away, heart thundering.

Forcing calm, she offered a weak small. "Nothing's bothering me."

"You're an awful liar, Chrissy."

Squaring her shoulders, she turned to grab her reticule. "I'm not lying. Come on, Cici. We need to get home."

"Ah, Chrissy. Can't we stay a little longer?" One look from her older sister had her clamping her mouth shut. "Oh…all right."

"I'll get Lucy tomorrow, unless…" Her voice trailed off when he held up both hands in an offer of surrender.

"As long as you stay for supper." When she went to object, he shook his head. "We all enjoy you and Cici being here, Chrissy."

"Can we, please?" Cici looked at her, hope shining in her bright eyes.

She hated saying no when there was no reason to stay home. "All right, we'll stay tomorrow. But don't expect it every night."

"Absolutely not." Hex smirked, his voice betraying his thoughts. "I'll walk you home."

"Me, too!" Lucy grabbed her father's hand.

She eyed him with suspicion. He often walked them to the boardinghouse, but hadn't expected it once she and Cici had moved. "It's not necessary, Hex."

"I'm not letting you walk home alone. You girls ready?"

At their nods, he opened the back door, ushering them outside. They walked four abreast, the only sounds coming from Ruby's Palace and the occasional shout from Frontier Street.

"You should hold Chrissy's hand, Papa."

Glancing down at Lucy, he smiled. "You're right." Reaching out, he threaded his fingers through Christina's, surprised when she didn't pull away. She didn't look at him either, keeping her focus straight ahead.

They'd made it to her front door before she tugged her hand free. The lack of contact jolted him for a moment, a sensation he'd never felt before tonight. By the look in her eyes, she felt the same sense of loss.

"You ladies—" Hex spun at gunfire from Frontier Street, pulling his gun from its holster. "Get the girls inside!" Several more shots ripped through the night air. "Now!"

Jerome Taggert slipped between two buildings, spitting mad at the appearance of his twin brothers. He'd ordered Theo and Byron to wait for him in camp. Both of them showing up now made his job more difficult.

He'd waited outside the St. James over an hour for the Groom family to return. The son and daughter arrived a few minutes before Ma and Pa, taking the steps into the hotel.

Before he could follow them inside, a commotion came from Finn's, the new saloon a few buildings away. Shots were fired. Two men, then another two, flew out the front doors, tumbling into the street. The turmoil continued, as did the gunfire from rowdy onlookers before deputies took over.

That's when Jerome saw his brothers. The fight could've been the perfect cover for rushing inside the hotel, retrieving the money from Pa Groom, and getting out of town while the deputies were otherwise occupied.

Instead, Theo and Byron were on one side of the scuffle while Jerome was hidden outside the St. James. They couldn't afford to be seen or recognized. Although the chance of anyone connecting them with the shooting at the boardinghouse was remote, Jerome wasn't taking any chances.

Cursing, he motioned for them to join him. Hurrying behind the buildings, they came up beside their brother, guns held to their sides.

Jerome whirled to face his brothers. "What the hell? I told you to stay at camp and wait for me."

Sheepish expressions appeared before Theo spoke. "We couldn't let you ride in alone. If anything happened, how would we know about it?"

"Doesn't matter. This was about keeping you two out of this."

Byron shook his head. "We're already in this up to our necks. Besides, who is going to recognize us? We wore masks at the restaurant."

"They know there were three of us. We can't be seen together." Jerome blew out a stream of curses as he looked around the corner to where the deputies were leading several men to the jail. "The man who hired us is in his hotel room. I'm going to speak with Pa Groom about our money. I want you to find your horses, and head back to camp."

Theo's jaw worked, eyes hard with determination. "We aren't leaving you here. The deputies are out because of the brawl at Finn's. They're already watching for any other threats. Groom isn't going to go down without a fight. If he doesn't intend to pay us, you'll want to think this through, and include us in your plan to get what we're owed."

Jerome leaned his back against the outside wall of the hotel, scrubbing a hand down his face. He wasn't old. Not even thirty. A hard life and responsibility for his brothers had aged him sooner than most. He'd never had a relationship, friends, or respite from a life running from the law.

For years, Jerome had stared at the ceiling, trying to fall asleep with an empty stomach and no hope for the future. Whatever came their way, he split it between the three, giving Theo and Byron the most and taking leftovers for himself. Bone tired and unsure what to do next, he shoved away from the building.

"We'll ride back to camp. But hear me. This isn't over. We need the money, and I'm going to get the old man to pay up."

Chapter Thirteen

Hex helped Zeke, Shane, and Hawke secure the troublemakers in cells before leaving to claim his daughter. When first hearing the gunshots, his mind had gone back to the night of the shooting in the boardinghouse. Instead, it was a bunch of drunken cowboys. No injuries except for bruises, split lips, swollen eyes, and broken nose. That miscreant was already at the clinic.

"Unless you need my help, I'll be heading home." Shoving his hat farther down on his head, Hex headed outside. His gaze shot across and down the street to Finn's. The volume of the piano music had increased since the brawl, the flat sound of the chords making him cringe.

"Hello, Deputy."

Alana's voice sliced through him. He didn't have the energy or time to be genial with her tonight, nor did he have the desire. Fetching Lucy from Christina, a shot of whiskey, cup of coffee, and putting his feet up held priority for him right now.

Turning, he felt his body go rigid when she sidled up beside him, looping her arm through his. She wore a red velvet dress, cut low, decorated with ribbons and lace. He didn't want this, didn't want her.

Taking her hand in a firm grip, he slipped her arm from his, setting her aside. "I'm tired, and on my way home. You saw what happened earlier. It would be best if you got back to the saloon and stayed away from the street. I'm certain you have customers waiting."

She gripped his arm when he shifted to leave, running fingers up the front of his shirt. "Why don't you come by the saloon before going home? I'll buy you a drink. Two, if you'd like."

Gently shackling her wrists with his hands, he lowered them to her sides. "Not tonight, Alana. I'll come by when I have time." Releasing his grip, his hard gaze pinned her in place. "You're a beautiful woman. Most men would be happy with you by their side."

She lifted her chin, lower lip jutting out in more of an invitation than pout. "Not you?"

He shook his head. "Not me."

"Do you already have a woman, Hex?"

Instead of answering, he took another glance up and down the street. Seeing nothing of concern, he whirled on his heel and left.

"Someday, you'll regret not taking me up on my offer," she called after him.

Hex didn't know which offer she referred to, deciding it had to be the whiskey as he rounded the corner toward Christina's.

Christina rested her back against the headboard of her bed, her sister on one side, Lucy on the other. Both had fallen asleep after listening to a single story. She hesitated to move, not wanting either to wake up.

She groaned at the sharp knock on the front door. Waiting until the knock came again, she set the book aside, carefully sliding between the girls and off the bed.

Drawing open the door, she released a relieved sigh. Hex stood on the other side of the threshold, hat in his hand. "Sorry it's so late."

She stepped aside, motioning for him to come inside. "No problem at all. Is everyone all right?"

Gunfire always concerned Gabe, his deputies, and the townsfolk. It was too easy for innocent passersby to be hit by a misdirected bullet. Several bodies buried in the local cemetery were victims of too much liquor and short tempers.

"Drunken cowboys got into a fight. We took one of them to the clinic and locked up the others." Looking toward the kitchen, a sheepish grin brightened his face. "Do you have any coffee?"

"It'll take only a few minutes to make some."

"I don't want to put you out, Chrissy. I'm sure there's still some at home."

"Nonsense, Hex. I'd enjoy a cup, also." She was already walking past him toward the stove. It didn't take her long to start a new pot. "The girls are asleep. Took just one story."

"Luce usually insists on at least two." He watched her move about the kitchen, the graceful, efficient movements, and gentle sway of her hips.

Much of the strawberry-blonde hair tucked into a neat bun had come loose, strands falling to frame her heart-shaped face. Round, sparkling green eyes showed a combination of innocence and humor.

Taking the cup of coffee offered, he took a sip, continuing to watch her lithe, lush body move about the room. He found his breaths stuttering at the sight. How had he not recognized the depth of her beauty until now?

Chrissy sat down close to him, blowing on her coffee before taking a swallow. "Will the men in jail go to trial?"

"It's doubtful. They got into a fight and didn't do much damage. According to Doc McCord, the man with the broken nose is going to heal. Gabe will fine them enough to pay for the broken chairs and tables and warn them future brawls will mean longer jail time. Those boys can't afford to get fired from their ranch jobs." He took a critical look around. "Where did you get the new furniture?"

"From Noah. He let me go through his storage cabin. The chair you're sitting in and the one I'm using were delivered early this morning. I still need another table and sofa. Unless I travel to Big Pine, it's going to take some time."

"Chrissy, if you want to go to Big Pine, I'll take you. Anytime you want. We can ask Isabella to watch the girls while we're gone, or we can leave early on a Saturday and return on Sunday."

She tightened her grip on the cup, not sure what he was suggesting. "Are you saying we'd spend the night in Big Pine?"

"It's the only way to do it. It's close to four hours using a wagon. Five if we return with a full load. Which is the entire point of going there. Right?" He smiled, taking another small sip from his cup, trying to make it last.

Hex found he didn't want to leave. He wanted a nice house that turned into a home when Christina graced the interior. The thought hit him as if he'd been slammed with a wood plank. He wanted her with a force that scared him. Wanted her in his life, his home, his bed. Not for a night or two, but for the rest of his life.

"Hex, are you all right?"

He hadn't realized his mind had wandered so far away, into a future he had no right to expect. "Yes, I'm fine." Finishing his coffee, Hex stood, knowing he had to get out of there before saying something he wasn't ready to admit. "I should take Lucy home."

"I'll get her." She began to push out of her chair, stopping when he held up his hand.

"No need." Entering the bedroom, he stopped, taking a quick look around. A beautiful quilt graced the bed. Striking watercolors of birds and flora hung on the walls. The smell of woman permeated the air, making him tighten with desire. He really did need to head home.

Scooping Lucy from the bed, he held her close to his chest as he walked into the living room and toward the door. "Thank you again, Chrissy."

She had no time to reply before they disappeared outside.

Shane could see the accident coming before the young woman realized what was happening. Rushing across the street, he waved his arms in warning. An instant before the out-of-control wagon careened toward her, Shane grabbed her around the waist, jumping onto the boardwalk. The wagon flew by, the young driver yelling for people to get out of the way.

Setting her down, he looked her over, seeing no bruises or scratches. "Are you all right, miss?"

Swiping hair from her face, she straightened her dress and hat before meeting his gaze. "I believe so. A little shaken maybe. I'm Christina McKenna."

He removed his hat, making a slight bow. "Deputy Shane Banderas."

"Oh. I heard you are one of two deputies Gabe hired."

"You heard correctly, Miss McKenna. I'm on my rounds. May I escort you someplace?"

Feeling her face heat, her gaze quickly moved over him. His skin was the golden brown of those who worked outside. The soft chambray shirt stretched across a hard chest, his muscled arms straining the fabric. He'd pulled his silky auburn hair into a queue at the nape of his neck. And his eyes. She could get lost in the pools of soft green, so much like her own.

"I was on my way to Allie Coulter's dress shop. It's near the bank."

"Yes, I've heard of her from Cash."

"Her husband," she commented.

He nodded, slipping her arm through his. "Perfect. I'm headed in the same direction."

Heat pooled in her stomach, growing when her hip brushed his as they began to walk. She'd never had a man show such immediate interest in her. The attention was flattering after having Hex ignore her for so long. Well, not necessarily ignore, but he'd certainly never seen her as a woman who'd interest him. It felt good to be noticed.

"How long have you been in Splendor, Miss McKenna?"

"Just over a year."

"What are your thoughts?"

"If you're referring to the town, I love it. In a short time, it's become home to me and my younger sister, Cecilia. And you?"

"I'm a wanderer. I heard through a lawman in Wyoming about Gabe looking for more deputies. I'd delivered some prisoners to Deer Lodge and decided to ride through on my way south. I liked what I saw and heard. Sheriff Evans is a persuasive man."

"A good, honest man, too." She'd believed in him since the first time they met, soon after arriving in Splendor.

He tried to slow his pace, but before he was ready to let her go, they stood in front of Allie's shop. "Here you are."

"Thank you, Deputy Banderas. You are wonderful company."

A tight smile formed before he made a quick decision. "If you have no plans for lunch, may I escort you to the restaurant at the boardinghouse? You can tell me more about Splendor and the people."

The invitation caught Christina by surprise. Excitement coursed through her at sitting at the table with the quite handsome, new deputy. Hex crossed her mind, but the image faded at the expectant look on Shane's face.

He was a stranger who'd decided to stay for a while in the town she'd grown to love. Sharing lunch, explaining about Splendor and its people would be doing him a service. Christina couldn't think of one reason not to spend an hour with him.

"Having lunch with you would be lovely."

A small smile broke across Shane's face.

She felt a surge of long lost confidence, her smile matching his. "What time shall I meet you there, Deputy?"

"Noon, Miss McKenna." He touched the brim of his hat. "I'll look forward to it."

Me, too. She watched him walk off before turning to enter the dress shop.

Chapter Fourteen

Hex leaned against the outside corner of the jail, hat pushed back on his forehead as he scanned the street. Ever since the shooting in the boardinghouse, he'd been trying to ignore the uneasy feeling the danger wasn't over.

He'd lain awake at night trying to identify the reason for his concern, coming up with nothing. During daylight, Hex did his best to hunt down the cause while performing his job as a deputy. Now his eyes widened.

Across the boardwalk, he spotted Shane coming his way, his features relaxed, mouth curved into an almost imperceptible smile. He couldn't remember seeing the new deputy with anything other than a slight scowl or neutral expression.

Hex thought of Christina, wondering where she was, what she was doing. At almost noon, she could be visiting one of her many friends or shopping for supper. She'd joined a quilting group including Gabe's wife, Lena, and Nick Barnett's wife, Suzanne, plus several other women who'd settled in Splendor over the last few years.

Feeling the need for a cup of coffee, he shoved from the wall, stopping when Christina emerged from the gunsmith shop next door.

Her smile was tight, steps faltering when she saw Shane across the street. "Hello, Hex."

"How are you today, Chrissy?" His features softened, as they did so often when he spoke to her.

"I'm well. You?"

"Fine."

After their relaxed conversation the night before, her clipped responses surprised him. "Are you certain you're all right?"

Christina switched from one foot to another, watching Shane head into the boardinghouse. "I'm a little late for a lunch appointment is all. I'll get the girls and have supper fixed by the time you're home." She flushed at the slip. "I mean...when you're done for the day. Well, I'll see you in a few hours."

He stayed on the boardwalk another minute as she crossed the street and entered the boardinghouse, then began another turn around town. It took almost forty-five minutes to return to Frontier Street and stop in front of the boardinghouse.

Glancing inside, his jaw clenched. At a table near the back, Shane and Christina were in deep conversation. He didn't know how and when they'd met, as the deputy had begun his position earlier that week. The man sure moved fast.

Disgusted, he tried to contain his jealousy, an emotion new to him. He didn't like the feeling one bit. Storming down the boardwalk, he barely spoke to those he passed as he struggled with the possibility Christina could hold an interest in another man. He'd thought there would be more time for courting, see if they might have a future together. First, he actually had to show his interest, as Shane may have already done.

Reaching Finn's, Hex slowed his pace. He'd passed by the new saloon several times since it opened, never going inside. Not even the night of the brawl. Stopping by the door, he peered inside. Early afternoon and the place was quiet.

His gaze scanned the large room, hoping Alana was nowhere about. The last person Hex wanted to see was the woman who continued to throw herself at him. Besides, he wouldn't be staying more than a few minutes.

"Deputy Boudreaux, you finally decided to come for a visit."

He inwardly groaned at the familiar voice. Instead of moving toward her, he retreated. Hex saw today she'd dressed in a simple cotton dress, which appealed to him much more than velvet and lace and bright red lips. Still, the woman would never be the equal of Christina.

"Miss Hanrahan. I'm making the rounds. Everything quiet in here?"

She swept her arm across the room. "Yes, but it *is* early in the day. I'm sure we'll need your help in a few hours." Alana's face fell in disappointment when he took another step away. "Aren't you coming in?"

"No, ma'am. I'm still on duty." *And trying to cool my simmering temper.* He hadn't been able to get the sight of Christina with Shane out of his mind. It was a situation he needed to take care of right away. "Good day, Miss Hanrahan."

She didn't try to stop him, for which he was grateful. The temptation to walk back to the boardinghouse overwhelmed him, but he ignored the desire, heading for Splendor's growing Chinatown.

It wasn't far away, a short two blocks. Grant Street had been named at the request of those owning businesses and living on the block. All the shops had apartments on the second floor, a few with three stories. The storekeepers sold meat, fish from nearby rivers and lakes, herbs, medicines, books, silk fabric, and a large general store selling tobacco, staples, candy, clothing, and hats. Many non-Chinese frequented these shops, making Grant Street an important part of Splendor's economy.

Before he reached the street, the scent of smoke hit him. His solid pace changed to a run as he sought the source of what had to be a fire. Halting at one end of Grant, he froze at the sight of thick, dark gray smoke pushing out of a building at the far end of the street. Several people filled buckets, throwing the contents at the fire. Hex knew it wouldn't be enough.

Turning, he ran back to the jail, shoving the door open to see Gabe, Mack, Caleb, and Hawke. "There's a fire in Chinatown."

Nothing more needed to be said before they hurried from the jail, each running toward the fire. It took little time to assess the direction the fire moved. Gabe began to direct people in forming bucket brigades coming from two directions.

"Caleb. Go to the livery and alert Noah."

After a quick nod to Gabe, he was gone. More people showed up, jumping in to offer their help. The biggest concern continued to be the fire spreading to other buildings. With everything made of wood, and most contents flammable, frontier structures didn't take long to burn down.

"Hex. Keep the people away from the blaze unless they're on that end of the bucket brigade."

"Will do."

The rest of his deputies, Beth Evans, Gabe's sister-in-law, Beau, Cash, Zeke, Shane, and Dutch McFarlin, who'd recently returned from a trip into Idaho, all arrived within minutes of each other.

Gabe continued to pump water into buckets while barking orders. "We've got to stop it before it destroys more businesses."

They'd lost the building where they believed the fire started, plus the vegetable market, then watched in horror as the flames licked the wooden side of the meat market.

More people arrived, two additional bucket brigades organizing without orders. The original shouts settled to muffled determination between townsfolk over a common goal of saving Chinatown.

Noah arrived in a wagon with four barrels filled with water. Too quickly, the barrels were empty. In less than thirty minutes, one side of the block lay in ruins. The one blessing was the opposite side of the street hadn't been touched by the fire.

Beth Evans stood listless, watching the flames die out, embers crackling. "We weren't able to save any of it, Gabe."

Shirt covered in soot, he put an arm around her. "One side of the street is still intact, and we stopped it from progressing to other blocks. We were able to accomplish a great deal, Beth. Our job now is to encourage them to rebuild."

"Do you doubt they will?"

"Not for a minute. With help, they'll be back in business within weeks. I'm going to establish more frequent patrols to keep thieves away. Not that there's much to steal." Gabe looked at the smoldering embers, studied the stricken faces of the shop owners who gaped at all they'd lost. "They're resilient." The comment was more to convince himself than state a fact.

"I remember when there was a fire in New York's Chinatown. Within a month, burned out shops were back to full operations, with families living above them. If you don't object, I'm going home to clean up before going to the jail."

Gabe's gaze scanned the crowd, surprised at some of the people who'd volunteered. Ruby Walsh, the owner of the Palace, brushed dirt from her dress with little success. Beside her were several of the girls who worked for her.

Close by, Stan Petermann, owner of the general store, spoke with the bank president, Horace Clausen, and Reverend Edward Paige. All had their sleeves rolled up, clothes dirty from helping to douse the fire. As Gabe watched, he recognized several other businessmen who joined them. Men who'd worked beside their Chinese neighbors to save the buildings.

Hex and Zeke came to stand by Gabe and Beth, their clothes and faces covered in dirt and soot. Neither said anything, concentrating on the destruction and the people. Gabe looked at them.

"Let's gather up the other deputies and meet at the jail. We've a lot of work to plan."

Pa Groom and Junior stood far enough away to watch the action but not be seen. They didn't speak, taking in the panic and hard work to extinguish the fire.

"This is good for us, Junior."

"How do you figure?"

"The sheriff and his deputies will be focused on the rebuilding, their attention drawn away from us."

Junior's spirits rose. "We're leaving?"

Pa looked at him, his expression neutral. "Not yet."

"How much longer are we going to be stuck here? We need to move on."

Pulling a cigar from a pocket, he bit off one end, settling it between his lips without lighting it. "Patience, son. Their attention is somewhere else, giving us other opportunities."

Junior fell silent, considering what his father said. The older Groom had always been a man of few words, but the family took those words seriously. "What do you have planned?"

Pa stroked his short beard, his attention on the sheriff. "I'm still thinking on it."

Junior had become more vocal in his opposition to his father's sluggish deliberation. He and Sissy were more than ready to leave, build their own life without the interference of his parents. To do that, they needed several more big hauls, which couldn't be planned in Splendor.

Frustrated, Junior turned to face his father. "How soon until you arrive at a decision?"

He cocked a brow, paying no attention to the irritation in his son's voice. "Don't know. You can't rush a decision as important as this."

Pa looked up to see Gabe and two of his deputies watching them. The sheriff didn't move, but the scrutiny bothered Pa. Anytime lawmen found him or his family interesting, he developed a bout of hives, which lasted until he'd put a good deal of miles between them.

"Let's go." Pa turned, moving at a fast clip back to the hotel. "We have details to work out. The community festival is a week away."

Junior picked up his pace to keep up with his father. "What does the festival have to do with us?"

Taking the steps to the St. James two at a time, Pa went straight upstairs, Junior right behind him. When they reached the elder Groom's room, his father disappeared inside, leaving his son to stare at a closed door.

Chapter Fifteen

The following morning, Gabe took charge of finding the cause of the fire. All deputies except Zeke, Shane, and Hawk, who'd guarded the town overnight, met at the jail, as did Noah, Horace Clausen, Stan Petermann, Gabe's business partner, Nick Barnett, and Gabe's brother, Chan Evans, a U.S. Marshal.

"Any idea what caused the fire?" Stan leaned against the wall, rubbing his forehead.

"I walked through the debris late last night with Noah. With only lanterns for light, we didn't find much. We'll be doing a thorough inspection today, with the help of the deputies."

Nick fingered his mustache. "Could it have been set?"

"That's what Noah and I believe. The fire started in a building with a wood-burning fireplace in the front of the building. The owner said the fire started at the back. The shelves in the back held herbs in glass jars."

"The shelves were made of wood?" Hex asked Gabe.

"Yes. According to the owner, the items on them weren't flammable. Even so, the fire spread quickly. No paint or oil for lamps, which makes me wonder..." He shot a look at Noah.

"We'll go through the rubble, try to find anything that could've been used to start the fire."

"It's all burned, how will that help?" Horace asked.

Noah rested his hip on the edge of Gabe's desk, crossing his arms. "My pop and I built buildings along the docks where we lived. When there was a fire, we did all we could to determine the cause. I learned a great deal from the local firemen. We'll see if it's enough to learn anything about this fire."

Gabe leaned back in his chair, a smile tipping the corner of his mouth. "Why don't you tell them about what we discussed last night?"

"I've been planning to build a fire engine for quite a while now. Been reading about the ones back east. After last night, I believe it's time."

Horace's interest rose at the idea. "What are you thinking, Noah?"

"There's this company in Manchester, Vermont. They build horse-drawn, steam-powered fire engines. I'd pattern ours after the ones they offer, making adjustments for our needs."

"How long would it take to build it, and how much will it cost?" Nick asked.

"With my regular work, at least three months."

"And if you have help?" Stan asked.

"If there's someone I can depend on, six to eight weeks." Noah provided an estimate of cost. "I can make a more detailed list for you."

Gabe drummed fingers on the desk. "Splendor is growing with no end in sight. Yesterday's fire could've destroyed all of Chinatown, spread to the Palace, and continued down that block. If so many people hadn't shown up, we'd be looking at a great deal more rebuilding. And we were lucky this time. No one died and the injuries were minimal, limited to slight burns by some of those who came to help. Next time, our luck may not hold."

"Everything Noah and Gabe have said makes a great deal of sense," Nick said. "I believe the town should agree to provide the funds and a workman of Noah's choice to build a steam-powered fire engine." He lifted a brow at the others. "Gentlemen?"

Horace nodded. "I'd like to see a list of costs. Assuming it's within reason, I'm agreeable to it."

"I agree it's time the town added a fire engine, and Noah's the best person to build it," Stan said.

Gabe cleared his throat. "I'm also in agreement. Now, let's get started on finding the cause of yesterday's fire."

It had been two long days for Christina. She'd kept the girls away from the fire while preparing to leave the house if they were unable to contain it. Thank goodness, evacuating wasn't necessary.

Going to bed close to one in the morning, she woke to find Hex had never come by to check on Lucy. She assumed he'd worked late, collapsing in his own bed before starting again the following morning.

Hex knocked on her door close to midnight on the second day, tired legs taking him inside to collapse on one of her overstuffed chairs. He'd stopped by his place long enough to clean up, eat a bowl of stew, and down a shot of whiskey.

"I didn't think you'd come by tonight, Hex." Christina sat across from him, noting the additional lines around his eyes, the exhaustion on his face. "The girls fell asleep hours ago. It took a while to get them settled after what happened in Chinatown. Was anyone hurt?"

Resting his head against the back of the chair, Hex let out a slow breath. "A few injuries and wounds, but no deaths." Closing his eyes, he fought the urge to fall asleep, unaware he'd lost the battle until he woke after sunrise, a blanket draped over him from neck to his boots. Wincing at the painful crick in his back and neck, his eyes opened to slits.

"What the..." Hex's voice trailed off as recognition came in small bits. He'd fallen asleep in Christina's living room. Before he had a chance to stand, young voices came from Cici's bedroom. The door flew open, the girls rushing out, only to come to a stop.

Lucy's eyes burst wide. "Papa. What are you doing in a chair?"

"I must've fallen asleep."

She and Cici giggled, watching him rub his eyes and unfold his long body out of the chair. The door to the second bedroom opened. Christina hesitated a moment before joining the others in the living room.

"You were so peaceful, I didn't want to disturb you. Hope you slept all right."

"Fine," he ground out, massaging his neck.

Biting back a smile, she turned toward the kitchen. "I'll make coffee. Girls, would you please help with making breakfast? I have eggs and bacon, Hex."

"Anything sounds good to me, Chrissy. May I use your water closet?"

"Of course. Cici, please show Hex the water closet." Having their own toilet, sink, and bathtub had been what convinced her to rent the house from Noah. "We should have breakfast ready soon."

He followed Cici to the modest, yet well-appointed bathroom. She'd spent money on extra towels and soap, which he guessed came from the Splendor Emporium owned by Josie Lucero and Olivia McCord.

Finishing his business, Hex washed his hands before splashing water on his face. The actions helped him wake up. He had to get to the jail, start another day looking for who set the fire.

Their search of debris the day before had turned up three charred sticks. Two with scraps of material at one end, the last with an almost intact wad of cloth.

There was no doubt among those examining the torches they were what had been used to start the fire. Now they had to discover who threw them.

145

Returning to the kitchen, he inhaled the wonderful aroma of bacon, spotting a stack of flapjacks on the table. His mouth watered.

"Get some coffee and sit down, Hex. Cici and Lucy, take seats at the table. We have to leave in thirty minutes for school."

Filling his plate as well as the girls', he began to eat. "This is wonderful, Chrissy." She always amazed him at the ease with which she prepared a meal.

"I can make more if that's not enough."

"This will be enough, thanks. Luce, you need to keep eating so you aren't late for school."

"I'm eating as fast as I can, Papa." She shoved a small spoonful of eggs into her mouth.

Chrissy sat down next to him, picking at an egg and flapjack while taking quick glances at him. She'd eaten with Hex many times. Somehow, sharing a meal in the early morning felt more intimate, as if they were a family. How she wished they were.

"I've got to head to the jail. Thanks again for keeping Lucy, and for breakfast."

"Shall I keep her tonight?"

Hex strapped his gunbelt around his waist before settling his hat on his head. "Not unless something unexpected happens again. Until the shooting at the restaurant a couple weeks ago and fire the other night, it had been real quiet in Splendor."

"It will be again." She joined him at the door. "We'll be at your house when you're finished today."

Hex had the strangest urge to bend down and kiss her. Not on the cheek, but on her lush lips. It wasn't the first time he'd wanted to take her in his arms and discover what it would be like to hold and kiss her. He couldn't do it now, not in front of the girls, but he did have an idea.

"Chrissy, I want to take you to supper."

"You just took all of us out for my birthday, Hex."

"I don't want the others to come along. This supper will be the two of us. Do you know what I'm suggesting?"

Her heart began to beat in a rapid staccato rhythm. "I, um...am not sure."

Opening the door, he motioned for her to go out ahead of him, leaving the girls inside. He shut the door, placing his hands on her shoulders.

"I want to court you, Chrissy. That is, if you're interested."

She felt her jaw drop, her heart all but stop. "Court...me?" Chrissy barely got the words out. Never had she believed Hex would show this level of interest in her.

A small smile curved the corners of his mouth. "Is that so surprising?"

"Yes," Chrissy said before she could stop herself.

Chuckling at her honest response, he placed a finger under her chin, lifting her face to meet his. "It's true. Are you free on Saturday evening? I'll ask Isabella if she'd watch the girls."

She swallowed the growing lump in her throat, still having a hard time believing Hex Boudreaux held an interest in her. "Yes, I'm free."

"I'll make reservations for us at the Eagle's Nest. Shall I come by at six o'clock?"

Throat thick with excitement, eyes wide, she could only nod.

His lips twitched. "We can discuss it more at supper tonight at my place."

Clearing her throat, she nodded again. "I would like that, Hex."

"Good." This time he did bend down and brush a kiss across her cheek. "I'll see you tonight, Chrissy."

She couldn't get her legs to move, or stop watching the rugged lawman as he walked down the street toward the jail. His request had taken her by surprise. Even hearing his denial, Chrissy had been certain Hex held an interest in Alana.

A slow smile drew across her face as she pictured a life with Hex and Lucy. They'd live in town so he could keep his job as one of Gabe's deputies. She'd continue making meals, cleaning, and taking care of the girls.

Christina wondered if he'd want more children. Hex had Lucy and they'd be raising Cici. Maybe that would be enough for him. She knew it wouldn't be enough for her. Christina longed for children of her own, perhaps a boy or two who took after their father.

Laughter burst from her lips before she covered her mouth with a hand. Her yearning for a life with Hex had shifted into a fanciful, unrealistic dream.

He'd invited her to supper, nothing more. Yes, he'd talked of courting her, but did he mean it? Instead of wanting a life with her, was courting his way of thanking Christina for taking care of Lucy, cooking, and cleaning?

"Are we going to school?"

She whirled around at Cici's voice, momentarily forgetting the girls were waiting for her. "Of course. Are you ready?" Christina drew in a deep breath to clear the jumbled thoughts from her head.

In answer, Lucy and Cici rushed passed her to the street. Grabbing her shawl from inside, she hurried to catch up with them.

Christina walked between the two on the way to school. Instead of avoiding the fire's destruction, she purposely took a route which took them behind the destroyed buildings.

The girls stared, unusually quiet at what they saw. Their steps slowed as they skirted the charred remains of several buildings.

"Did anyone die, Chrissy?"

"Thankfully, no, Cici."

People worked among the wreckage, tossing aside materials no longer of use. Few looked up as they passed by, their focus on getting the block ready to rebuild. Christina spotted three deputies, Beau, Cash, and Dutch, working alongside others.

She also recognized the two men who'd been in the restaurant the night their tablemate had been shot. Something about their expressions caused her stomach to twist.

They weren't offering to help, choosing to watch others do the work. It didn't surprise her. After all, they had no connection to Splendor or its people. It was their hardened features, lacking any sign of empathy, which drew her attention.

The two men spoke to each other, not loud enough for anyone else to hear, though the intensity couldn't be missed. It seemed an odd reaction after such a terrible fire.

She made a mental note to mention the men to Hex. Their actions may mean nothing, but the churning in her stomach told her something quite different.

Chapter Sixteen

Hawke DeBell joined the other deputies working to clear the burned debris, his attention never leaving the two men leaning against the side wall of Ruby's Palace. He'd been watching them since arriving in town and taking the deputy job. All his instincts warned him they weren't as they appeared. After following them since arriving in town, he had nothing to go on except a hunch.

"We're forming a couple teams for the shooting competition. You interested?"

Hawke switched his gaze to Hex long enough to give a brisk nod. "I'll take a spot."

Slipping on gloves, Hex began picking up and tossing ruined boards aside. "We're going to meet Sunday after church to divide the teams."

"Haven't been to church in a long time. I don't know if your preacher will let me inside."

Hex chuckled. "You don't have to worry about Reverend Paige. He takes every kind of sinner." Seeing Hawke's attention on the two men outside the Palace, he straightened. "Do you still believe they're the men you've been hunting?"

"I've been watching them since arriving in town and I'm certain they're Pa and Junior Groom. Not surprising, the names they're using here are different.

And I'd never heard about them traveling with women until coming to Splendor."

"If you're so certain, let's get them to the jail so you can question them."

Hawke didn't respond right away, taking time to consider Hex's words as he continued to sort through wreckage while watching the men. He seemed in no hurry, knowing Gabe had warned them not to leave town. Hawke wondered how much longer they'd comply.

"Not yet. I want to watch them a little longer and figure out how the women are connected with Pa and Junior."

"Assuming they're the Grooms." Hex heaved a large column out of the way, his attention latching onto Christina as she passed the leveled block on her way back home. A smile appeared when she saw him.

"Nice lady."

Hex pulled his gaze from Christina to look at Hawke. "Yes, she is."

"Are you serious about her?"

"You got a reason for asking?"

"Curious is all." Hawke's attention returned to the Grooms, who were walking back toward Frontier Street.

Hex let Hawke's obvious interest in Christina go. He'd already made up his mind to court her, would be escorting her to supper at the Eagle's Nest on Saturday. He hoped it would be enough to warn other suitors away.

Removing his gloves, Hawke stuffed them in his back pocket, brushing both hands down his pants. "I'm going to follow them."

"If you believe they are the bank robbers you've been chasing, then they could've been behind the shooting of the man at the boardinghouse restaurant. They may also have hired the three men who did it. Speak with Gabe again, Hawke. I'll offer to help you follow them."

Before turning to leave, his fellow deputy nodded once, the grim expression saying more than any words.

Gabe shifted in his chair, rocking his infant daughter, Emma. His wife, Lena, had brought her by the jail late Saturday morning so she could go shopping. It wouldn't be a long trip, less than an hour. Still, it limited his ability to handle problems outside the jail. It also made him the center of attention when anyone stopped by.

Lena had been gone less than ten minutes when the door opened, Dax and Luke Pelletier entering. Huge smiles appeared on their faces at the sight of Emma. Grabbing chairs, they sat across the desk from Gabe.

"Whatever brought you to town must be important for both of you to leave the ranch."

Dax crossed his arms, leaning back in the chair. "Rustlers."

Gabe continued rocking Emma when the door opened. Dutch and Mack strolled inside, greeting the Pelletiers before sitting down.

Without explanation, Gabe's face sobered. "How many head?"

Mack and Dutch shot looks at the other men, but said nothing.

"A hundred head," Luke answered. "Until now, it's been a few head at a time, stolen every couple weeks. We couldn't find tracks to determine where they'd been taken. Bull and Dirk did the count together this week, and we've lost over fifty more head in the last three days."

"This time, we did find tracks and the trail they took," Dax said. "They're being driven south into Wyoming, toward Fort Laramie. We have men following them."

Luke leaned forward, resting his arms on the desk. "The significance of this is we lost a contract for supplying one hundred head to Fort Laramie and other Army outposts in Wyoming to a rancher in Idaho. We've been trying to learn more about him, but we've found nothing."

Gabe stood, cradling Emma in his arms as he walked back and forth in the jail. "You're suggesting the rancher doesn't exist."

"That's what we believe," Dax answered. "He's awarded an Army contract at a price considerably below market, steals the cattle, changes the brand, and fulfills the contract."

Mack blew out a breath, shaking his head. "A real slick con. Rustle cattle and deliver them to the Army as their own."

"We want them arrested, Gabe."

Shifting Emma, he rubbed the back of his neck. "If they changed the brand, can you prove they're your cattle, Dax?"

"Two of our men, Bull and Travis Dixon, got close enough to check the brand. They believe with a clean brand to show the difference, it should be enough to prove the hundred head are ours."

Gabe sat back down, pressing a kiss to Emma's forehead before resuming the rocking motion. "Shane knows Wyoming. He used to be a deputy in Cheyenne. Take him with you."

Dax and Luke exchanged glances. "Shane?" Luke asked.

"Shane Banderas. A new deputy, as is Hawke DeBell. You can have both accompany you."

"Banderas should be enough," Dax said. "We need to get going right away."

Mack stood, heading for the door. "I'll find Shane and send him back here."

Dax and Luke also stood, both holding out their hands to shake Gabe's.

"Don't do anything on your own. Let Shane work with the captain at Fort Laramie to figure this out. He'll arrest the men who stole the cattle, pay you, and none of your men will go to jail. Do you both understand?"

Smiles rolled across their faces, neither giving an affirmative nod.

Dax lingered a moment before leaving. "Thanks, Gabe. I'll send you a telegram when this is settled."

When the door closed behind them, Gabe turned to Dutch, who'd said nothing during the entire exchange. "I want you to go with them. Make certain none of the Pelletier men end up in jail...or worse."

"Yes, sir." A large, burly deputy with unruly red hair, Dutch was a man of few words and unerring actions. He seldom overindulged in alcohol, had never shown more than a slight interest in any woman, and kept to himself a good deal of the time.

"Thanks, Dutch. I appreciate it."

Rising, he waved a hand in the air. "Whatever you need, Gabe."

Watching Dutch leave, Gabe was overtaken by a powerful surge of doubt, a feeling so rare it unsettled him. The Pelletier men were the best cowhands and wranglers in Montana. He'd wager his own deputies were superior to most other lawmen in the west. Gabe had no reason to be uncertain about the cattle ownership.

Still, his gut churned, warning the outcome might be far from guaranteed.

Christina retrieved the girls from where they'd been playing next to the creek, anxious to get back to prepare supper for Zeke and the girls, then get ready for the evening with Hex. This time, she chose to take Frontier Street instead of walking by the burned buildings.

Cici and Lucy chattered as they passed one shop after another. Making a quick stop at the general store, they retraced their steps to pass between the barber shop and the gunsmith on their way to Rimrock Street and Hex's house.

The new route didn't allow them to avoid Chinatown. To her surprise, a great deal of cleanup had been completed since morning. Almost all the charred remains were gone, new lumber stacked around the perimeter. Men still worked, both shop owners from Chinatown and those outside the area.

"Christina!"

She turned at the familiar voice. "Frannie. It's good to see you."

"Are you headed home?"

"To the Boudreaux place to fix supper for Zeke and the girls. Hex is taking me to the Eagle's Nest tonight." She didn't attempt to hide her excitement.

Francesca's friendly expression froze. "That's wonderful."

"Why don't you join them for supper? I'm certain Zeke would be fine having you there." She looked ahead, motioning for the girls not to go any farther away.

"I guess Zeke hasn't said anything."

"Did something happen between the two of you?"

Wrapping arms around her waist, Francesca shook her head. "*Nothing* has happened. I haven't seen him since the night I had supper with all of you. Zeke had an appointment with me to discuss buying a parcel of land west of town. He didn't appear. That was a week ago and I've heard nothing from him."

Christina placed a hand on her friend's arm. "I don't know what to say. It's been obvious to Hex and me that Zeke is taken with you."

A bitter chuckle crossed Francesca's lips. "Not anymore. It's all right, though. I need to concentrate on building my law practice. There isn't much time to have a relationship."

Christina knew how Francesca felt. After seeing Hex enjoy Alana's company, she'd all but given up ever having him show an interest in her.

"There are also a good number of single men in Splendor. Have you met the two new deputies?"

Francesca held up a hand. "I'm not interested in meeting anyone right now, Chrissy."

"Still, you should know about them. I mean, you're a lawyer and they're lawmen."

Chuckling, Francesca relented. "All right. Tell me their names, but nothing else. As I said, there truly is no time to show an interest in a man, no matter how spectacular he is."

Christina shot another look at the girls to make certain they stayed close. "Shane Banderas and Hawke

DeBell. Hex thinks a great deal of both." She wanted to say more, but stopped when Francesca shook her head, holding up her hand a second time.

"Their names are enough, Chrissy. I should return to the office before going home." A small, wistful smile crossed her face before it faded as she turned to leave.

"Let's plan to have lunch next week, Frannie."

Shifting slightly, she nodded before continuing down the street.

Chapter Seventeen

Christina finished the last preparations for her evening with Hex. Smoothing her hands down a beautiful blue taffeta dress pulled from a trunk unopened since leaving Kansas City, she studied herself in the mirror.

Her body had matured since last wearing it before her father died. It draped over curves nonexistent a few years before, and she had to admit it looked better now. Christina hoped Hex would approve.

Cici and Lucy had eaten an early supper, leaving enough for Zeke when he stopped by before going to the jail. Afterward, she'd shuffled the girls to Isabella Dixon's house. With her husband, Travis, helping retrieve stolen Pelletier cattle, she was more than willing to watch the girls.

A soft knock on the door stilled nervous efforts at improving her appearance. Letting out a slow breath, she lifted the reticule from the dresser. She worked to control the fluttering in her stomach, the fear of disappointing Hex. Opening the door, she needn't have worried.

His expression, the way his breath caught for an instant, relieved her concern. "You look beautiful, Chrissy." His comment reassured her.

"Thank you, Hex. Would you like to come inside while I fetch my coat?"

He walked past her, leaving the door slightly ajar. Before tonight, he'd been inside her house only when others were around. Tonight, he felt a tinge of unease at being alone with her without a chaperone.

No matter her maturity or beauty, Hex still had visions of her as younger, clinging to her dying twin, Millie, tears streaming down her cheeks. As others had said, Christina was no longer that girl. Instead, she was a resilient, strong woman. Someone to respect for her own accomplishments, loyalty, and commitment to her young sister.

"I'm ready." She stood before him, waiting.

It took Hex a few long moments to hold out his arm so she could slip hers through. "Would you like to take a walk around town before supper?"

"Would it be rude of me to say I'm starving and would rather walk afterward?"

He threw back his head and laughed, delighted with her honesty. "Afterward is fine, Chrissy."

They walked in silence to the Eagle's Nest, greeting the few people still out at this time of evening. Never since her mother died had she felt special, been treated as someone of importance to another person.

When her father remarried, it was to a young and shrewish woman who sought only his wealth. She'd treated her two stepdaughters with little regard. It was hard to understand how such a wonderful child as Cici had been born to such a cold, selfish woman. Moving west after their deaths had been a somewhat rash but good decision. Even with Millie gone, Chrissy was glad they'd left the bittersweet memories behind.

"Good evening, Deputy Boudreaux." Thomas, who'd served as the concierge since the hotel and restaurant opened, smiled broadly.

"Hello, Thomas."

Christina nodded at the still young man, unable to squelch a grin.

"We have the table you requested. Please, follow me."

The table was perfect. Located by the front window, a white cloth graced the top, along with two silver candlesticks with lit candles and a vase filled with flowers in the center.

"This is lovely, Thomas."

"Thank you, Miss McKenna. It took a bit to find flowers tall enough for the vase, and..." He flushed, realizing he'd said more than intended. Pulling out her chair, he waited until she was seated to hand each of them a handwritten menu before looking at Hex. "Would you like wine this evening?"

"Yes, we would."

"We have a red wine from Ohio."

"That would be fine, Thomas." Hex switched his attention to Christina, smiling at her wide eyes. "Have you ever had wine before?"

"I've had punch with wine in it, but never a glass. I'm certain I'll like it."

"If you don't, I'll order you something else." Lifting the menu, he scanned the offerings, settling on the goose with applesauce.

"Who hunts for the birds and game on their menu?" Christina's question was spoken so low Hex had to lean toward her, getting a whiff of her enticing perfume. Inhaling her unique scent, he hesitated before straightening in his chair.

"Gabe says they buy from various locals who bring in their game. You've met Baron Klaussner?"

"Yes, and his son, Johann. I'm told he has an enormous home outside of town."

"It's the biggest lodge I've ever seen. Gabe told me he provides a great deal of the meat offered. What are you having?"

She glanced down the menu once more, biting her lower lip. "The lamb with mint sauce. Oh, look. They have lemon meringue pie and éclairs. Do you think May Covington made them?"

His eyes glittered at the excitement in her expression. "Caleb's wife makes all the pastries and desserts for Eagle's Nest. If you want, you may have both. Even three if it will please you."

The heat in his eyes had her body stirring in a way she'd never experienced. Christina had experienced fluttering in her stomach, or a tightening in her chest when she'd been close or brushed against him. This was different. His intense scrutiny made her squirm in her seat, swallow an unfamiliar wave of wanting she couldn't describe.

"Um, I believe three would be too many."

"Then we can share, Chrissy."

Once the server poured wine and took their orders, Hex settled back in his chair, doing his best not to stare at the stunning woman next to him. Sometime over the last few weeks, she'd come to mean more to him than just the friend who helped with his daughter.

He hid a smile when she took a sip of the red wine, winced, then swallowed. "What do you think?"

She took another sip, let it roll down her throat, not showing any reaction this time. Choking, she touched the napkin to her lips. "It may take me some time to acquire a taste for it."

Chuckling, he reached over and patted her back. "Not unusual."

Christina took one more sip, her eyes sparking as if remembering something.

"Has Zeke decided he no longer holds an interest in Francesca?" The instant the words were out of her mouth, Christina winced. It wasn't her business. "Never mind. Forget I asked."

Hex studied her for a moment, taking a sip of wine as he considered her question. "Zeke has said nothing to me about Francesca."

"As I said, forget I asked. Besides, there are a number of single men who will step forward knowing Zeke no longer cares for her."

Although Zeke's possible defection surprised him, his brother and Francesca weren't who he wanted to discuss on his first night of courting. "You're right, there are. The same as there are a number of single men interested in you, Chrissy."

Setting down her glass, her brows drew together. "Truly?"

He chuckled. "Does that please you?"

"Surprises me, which it shouldn't. Splendor is a town with many single men and few available women." She stopped herself from admitting only one man interested her.

Hex had been the only one to hold her interest since insisting the three girls travel by stage from Big Pine to Splendor. He'd been there for them, helped the girls settle in the frontier town, and introduced them to the townsfolk. Over the months, she'd fallen in love with the somewhat taciturn lawman.

Their conversation stalled as they ate their main courses, making only the occasional comment. As the plates were removed, Hex gave the server their order for dessert.

"Éclairs, lemon meringue pie, and almond cake with maple frosting."

The man's eyes widened. "All three, sir?"

"All three. And coffee." He looked at Christina. "Unless you'd prefer tea."

"Coffee is fine." She bit down on her lip so as not to laugh. When the server left, she shifted toward him, lying a hand on her stomach. "Three desserts?"

He shrugged, lips twitching. "We have all night to finish them."

"All night?"

He didn't respond right away, allowing the server to set the desserts between them and pour coffee.

"Will there be anything else, sir?"

Hex and Christina looked at each other and laughed. The server waited a few seconds before shaking his head and leaving them alone.

To both of their surprise, they finished all three desserts, leaving not even a crumb. Taking her hand, Hex escorted her down the steps of the St. James to the boardwalk before offering his arm.

"Walk with me?"

Sliding her arm through his, Christina nodded. "Please."

They said nothing at first, passing the Emporium, the noise of Finn's Saloon, where she dared a glance inside. "Have you been inside yet?"

"For a few minutes. I prefer the Dixie and Wild Rose."

She looked up at him, brow lifting. "Why?"

"The company. I prefer the people who work at those saloons over Finn's."

She wondered if he meant the girls providing entertainment. The thought of him with other women knotted her stomach. Christina knew many single men availed themselves of the services of the saloon ladies.

He tugged her close to his side. "No, Chrissy. I've never been entertained by the women in Splendor saloons."

She gasped, wondering if he'd read her mind. "How did you..." She didn't finish, feeling her face flush.

"I know you well enough to guess what you would be thinking."

"Not ever?" Christina asked.

"Not in Splendor. I have had women, Chrissy. And there's Lucy's mother. As you already know, Alice and I were never married." He continued along the boardwalk, ready to leave the subject behind.

Hex continued past the boardinghouse toward the creek. The sound of rushing water gave a soothing feel to the night. A single bench had been placed near the bank by Noah a few years before, allowing many to enjoy the creek both day and night. Some used it for fishing, others for solitude, many couples for time alone together. He motioned for her to sit down before he took the space beside her.

"Sometimes, I bring the girls here after school and let them play. They love throwing rocks into the creek and gathering flowers growing by the bank." She didn't hide her excitement of being so close to Hex, snuggling against his side.

Placing an arm over her shoulders, his hand rubbed her arm, glad no one else was about. "Luce loves all activities outside. I'm afraid my daughter often acts more as a boy than a girl."

"She's a wonderful child, Hex. She'll grow out of boyish games at some point. Cici is starting to ask about sewing and needlepoint. It will happen with Lucy."

Their conversation slowed, the night shrouding them in darkness, both enjoying their closeness. Christina knew it was inappropriate to be out here alone, without a chaperone, but she didn't care. It seemed neither did Hex.

"Have you made a decision about staying in Splendor?"

His question didn't surprise her, as she'd been wondering the same about him and Zeke. "I do love it here. The town and the people. I've made many friends in a short time, as has Cici. What about you, Hex?"

Tightening his arm around her, Hex let out a slow breath. Until now, he hadn't been sure about what he wanted. He no longer suffered from indecision. He whispered his response against her ear.

"I'll be staying, Chrissy."

Chapter Eighteen

Stretching her arms toward the ceiling, Christina let out a long, satisfied sigh. She didn't open her eyes right away, preferring to linger on the image in her head when coming awake.

Hex, smiling, his arm over her shoulders. Her stomach fluttered as it had last night. It had been the best evening of her life.

After walking her home, he'd brushed a kiss across her lips, lingering a moment longer than necessary. The second best part of the evening occurred a moment before he left. Hex had asked if she and Cici wanted to ride with him and Lucy after church on Sunday.

Sunday! That's today!

Christina jumped out of bed at the same time she heard a knock on the door. Grabbing her shawl off a chair, she rushed from her room, drawing open the door. Lucy ran inside ahead of Cici while Isabella stayed on the stoop.

"I'm so sorry. I must've slept in."

The older woman's kind smile relaxed her. "It's fine, Chrissy. I enjoy having them. They're all ready for church. With Travis away, would you mind if I went with you?"

"Not at all. Hex is coming by, so we'll all go together." She looked down at her bedclothes, flushing. "Do you mind watching the girls while I get dressed?"

"Of course. I'll make coffee while waiting."

With a grateful smile, Christina hurried back to her room. She went through her morning ritual, wasting no time getting ready. Within minutes, she finished, meaning to head to Cici's room. Instead, she stopped in the living room. The girls were playing quietly on the floor, waiting for her to join them. Isabella sat in the rocking chair Christina had purchased from Noah, cradling a cup of coffee in both hands. Before she could pour herself a cup, a rap sounded on the door.

Nervous energy carried her across the room. Drawing in a steadying breath, she opened the door. Hex stood outside, looking every bit as handsome as the night before.

"Papa!" Lucy jumped up, running into his open arms. "I missed you. Did you know Mrs. Dixon is going with us to church? We had pancakes for breakfast. She read us *two* stories." She lowered her voice, motioning for him to bend down as Christina backed away to give them privacy. "Did you have fun with Chrissy?"

Glancing across the room at the woman whose image had kept him awake the night before, he nodded. "Yes, we did."

When he attempted to straighten, Lucy grabbed his coat, holding him down. "Maybe you should marry her," she whispered against his ear.

Chuckling, he continued to watch Christina, noticing a slight blush. "Maybe I should." Eyes wide,

Lucy's smile lit his world. "You can't tell anyone. It's a secret between us."

Nodding vigorously, she whirled around to rejoin Cici, the joy on her face obvious to all in the room. Christina had watched the exchange, followed by Lucy's delighted expression, and couldn't help wondering what the two had said.

"Are we ready to leave?" Isabella set her cup in the kitchen, joining them near the front door.

"We are. Come on, Cici." Christina took a hesitant glance at Hex, who waited for the girls and Isabella to leave before him. A glint in his eyes came a moment before he held out his hand.

"Walk with me, Chrissy."

It was exactly what she'd hoped. The two of them strolled hand-in-hand behind the girls and Isabella, talking between themselves about the afternoon he'd planned.

"After church, we'll go home to change clothes. I'll get the horses ready at Noah's while you, Cici, and Lucy retrieve the lunch I ordered from Suzanne."

"Where are we going?"

Tightening his fingers around hers, he watched the girls dance around Isabella as they walked down the street. "Have you heard of a place the locals call Mystery Mesa?"

She thought a moment before shaking her head. "Not that I remember."

"Noah told me about it a few months ago. Zeke and I rode out to see it." Hex glanced down at her. "It's beautiful on the mesa. Tranquil and isolated. There's a large flat area, with trees surrounding it on three sides and a steep drop off on the fourth. The view is incredible, the perfect spot for a picnic."

"It sounds wonderful, Hex."

"It is. We'll need to take coats. It's cold up there."

Late March in western Montana meant chilly days and nights, with the possibility of snow storms. Today was clear and warmer than normal.

Christina's eagerness grew as they continued to the church. "How long will we be gone?"

Hex's brows drew together. "Most of the day. Is that too long?"

Most of the day with Hex would never be too long. "Not at all."

As they approached the church, Hex squeezed, then let go of her hand, shifting her arm through his. It wouldn't be wise to attract too much attention. He'd prefer to go a while longer before signaling his serious interest in Christina. The woman he intended to marry.

From their dwindling stack of wood, Jerome Taggert added wood to the fire before adjusting the coffee pot on the heated rocks. Theo and Byron had ridden into town the day before, replenishing their shrinking supplies. While there, his brothers had spent time watching the Grooms, a job they'd been doing every couple days since the shooting at the boardinghouse.

Pa and Junior either stuck close together while around town or sequestered themselves inside the St. James with the two women. Along with the money they owed the brothers.

Most days, they took their meals at the Eagle's Nest. Expensive, but it kept them safe within the confines of a building with other people. Not a good situation when the Taggert boys needed the money for the job they'd handled for the Grooms.

Killing a U.S. Marshal from another state had been no easy task. He'd been on the trail of the Groom family for months. It had been an unusual assignment for the lawman from another area, but his boss in Washington D. C. decided Michael Mulvaney was the best man for the job.

He'd gotten close to the Grooms before they discovered his true identity. Hiring the Taggerts to rid him from their lives had been an easy decision. It had been a dangerous job, but the money had been much too good to ignore.

Their biggest concern was the four leaving town without paying. Byron and Theo were making certain that didn't happen.

When they returned to their camp the night before, they had nothing new to report about the Grooms. What they had heard about was the ranch rodeo set to take place the following Sunday. Most people in town would be at the Pelletier ranch. Not one of them believed the Grooms would be attending, which meant they might take the opportunity to leave Splendor.

Finishing his work stoking the fire, Jerome brushed his hands down his pants and straightened. Whirling at the sound of an approaching horse, he drew his gun, then relaxed.

Theo and Byron entered camp, a buck draped over the back of one of their horses.

"Appears you had good luck today." Jerome helped them release the animal and hang it from a nearby branch.

As his brothers dressed the deer, Jerome removed from the saddlebags what they needed to prepare the meat. Before he finished, the sound of laughter blew through the trees toward them.

With a quick flick of his wrist, Theo and Byron left the buck, mounted their horses, and quietly disappeared in the opposite direction. The timing was close. A minute later, two girls on horseback entered the camp, reining to a stop at the sight of Jerome.

Right behind them was a woman and a man he'd seen once in town. The two had been seated at a table the night he and his brothers had murdered the lawman.

"Sorry to intrude. I'm Hex Boudreaux and this is Miss Christina McKenna." He pointed to the girls. "That one is my daughter, Lucy, and the older girl is Christina's sister, Cici."

"Tim Jones. Hope it's no problem camping here." Jerome knew it wasn't, but preferred being as amicable as possible.

"As far as I know, this is open land. You'd have to check with Horace Clausen at the bank to make sure." Hex twisted in the saddle to see both girls staring at the animal. "Lucy, Cici, come back over this way."

"Just got that buck a bit ago. I can share some if you want it."

"That's kind of you, but we're heading away from town," Hex said as he looked around the camp. Something about the man caught his interest, as did the fact there were three bedrolls on the ground. "It's a lot of meat for one man."

Jerome hesitated a moment before grinning. It brightened his face without reaching his eyes. "I keep a tin salt. The meat will last me a long while."

All Hex's instincts told him the man was lying. A bad feeling grew in the center of his stomach. "Good luck to you. Let's get going, ladies."

"Nice to meet you, Mr. Jones," Christina called over her shoulder as they rode away.

Lifting a hand, Jerome waited until they were out of sight before lowering it. He let another few minutes pass before whistling to signal Theo and Byron it was safe to return.

"Who were they?" Theo asked.

"A man and woman with a couple kids out for a ride. Nothing to worry about."

Byron leaned forward in the saddle, watching the trail the four took away from their camp. "Want me to follow them?"

Jerome shook his head. "No. They aren't any danger to us. Finish up the buck and let's eat. We need to talk about getting our money from the Grooms."

Hex continued to glance over his shoulder until they reached Mystery Mesa. The sick feeling in his stomach plagued him the entire ride after leaving the man's camp. He'd questioned enough people to know when someone lied to him. Tim Jones definitely lied about being alone.

"This is even better than how you described it." Christina beamed, her enthusiasm shifting to the girls.

Dismounting, Hex helped all three to the ground, watching as they ran toward the edge. "Don't get too close. It might not be as stable as it appears."

Christina held out her arms, stopping them a few feet away from the rim as Hex suggested. They could still see the view without being in danger.

"Look, Lucy." Cici pointed across the chasm to the other side. "There's a waterfall."

"Papa! Look!" Lucy grasped his hand, dragging him closer. "See the waterfall?"

"I do, Luce. I've been here before with your Uncle Zeke."

She stared up at him, her lower lip jutted out. "How come you didn't bring me?"

"We rode up here before the snow started and haven't been back." Moving next to Christina, he threaded his fingers through hers. "Are you glad we came all this way?"

Her smile was all the answer he needed. "It's spectacular, Hex. I could stand here all day and enjoy it. The sunsets must be remarkable."

"When the weather warms, we'll come back and find out for ourselves." He squeezed her hand, not voicing his hope they'd be married by then.

"I'd like that."

Letting go of her hand, he turned to retrieve the food from their saddlebags. "Are you girls ready to eat?"

Lucy and Cici chattered throughout lunch, then ran off to explore the area with a warning to stay close. Hex and Christina didn't move from their spots on the blanket, enjoying their time alone.

"What did you think of Mr. Jones?"

Hex didn't want to scare her by explaining his concerns. After thinking through what he'd seen, and remembering the pair of matching six-shooters around his waist, he wanted to return with Zeke and at least one other deputy. Hex had a horrible sense he'd met the man before.

Chapter Nineteen

Christina invited Hex, Zeke, and Lucy for supper Sunday evening. To her surprise, and as much as he wanted to accept, Hex begged off. His mind couldn't move beyond the man he'd met south of town, along with the overpowering gut instinct Tim Jones wasn't traveling alone.

He'd been convinced the three men who'd killed Henry Steed hadn't left the area. Nor could he convince himself the two men and two women at the table didn't have some connection to the shooters. Hex had nothing to prove it, but each time he ignored his instincts, something bad happened.

"I'm concerned about the man we met today."

Her brows drew together. "Tim Jones? What are you concerned about?"

"Did you notice there were three bedrolls laid out?"

Mouth twisting as she thought about the camp and what she'd seen, Christina shook her head. "No, I didn't."

"Plus, I saw three tin cups near the campfire."

"Three bedrolls and three tin cups. That does seem odd."

"I'm sorry about supper, but I need talk to Zeke and a couple others. I want to ride back out before they break camp and disappear."

"It's all right, Hex. This is important. Maybe you'll find the men who murdered that poor man."

"I hope so." He started to turn away, then stopped. Facing Christina, he bent down, giving her time to shift away. Instead, she went on tiptoes, lifting her face in eager anticipation.

He pressed his mouth to hers before slipping a hand behind her neck. Drawing her to him, Hex kissed her long and deep, doing all he could to keep his desire under control. Reluctantly, he finally broke the kiss and straightened.

Letting out an unsteady breath, he stepped away. "I may be gone for quite a while."

She touched her lips before looking up at him. "I'll, um...take care of Lucy and take her to school. Do what needs to be done, Hex."

Brushing his fingers down her cheek, a small smile curved the corners of his mouth as his voice lowered. "Thank you."

Christina leaned against the front door as he departed, wishing he could've stayed while understanding the need to learn more about Jones and any companions. Again, her fingers went to her lips, a wave of heat warming her face.

She'd been kissed before by a young man her father hoped would consider marriage. They'd attended parties, suppers with friends, and walks in the park. He'd kissed her a few days before her father and stepmother died. She foolishly thought he might step forward to help them through the trying time. Instead, he'd backed away, attending the funerals for as short a time as propriety dictated before disappearing.

Christina hadn't missed him. In the time they'd been together, all he'd talked about was himself, his family's business, and his hobbies. She'd been surprised when he appeared at her front door the day she and her sisters planned to leave Kansas City.

His showing wasn't to say goodbye. Instead, he tried to convince them to stay. Her late twin, Millie, was certain it had to do with the depth of their wealth, which made marriage a more appealing option. Christina had politely told him goodbye, and never looked back.

She'd never been as pleased with her decision as now. Over their time in Splendor, she'd learned Hex was not only honorable, stepping into hard situations instead of backing away, but he had a deep love for his daughter and brother. People looked to him for help and advice.

He was a man she could love. Did love, if she were honest.

Standing at the door until he disappeared down the street, for the first time, Christina thought of the threat he might be facing on the trail. Jones hadn't seemed dangerous. She'd have thought nothing more about him if Hex hadn't mentioned the extra bedrolls and cups.

Closing the door, she noticed two of the people who'd been at the table the night the man had been shot. Instead of the young man being with his aunt, and the young woman with her uncle, the two strolled along the back street hand-in-hand. At one point, he pulled her closer to one of the buildings and kissed her before they continued along the street.

The familiarity surprised her. She'd understood they hadn't met until being introduced on the stagecoach. Granted, they'd been staying in Splendor for a few weeks. Still, it seemed too soon for them to be so intimate on the public street.

It made her wonder if the four were more familiar with each other than they wanted Gabe and his deputies to believe.

"Pa has something planned for the day of the ranch rodeo, Sissy. He won't tell me what, but I have a good idea." Junior tugged her inside one of the unoccupied houses Noah had built not far from Christina's place, closing the door quickly.

"What do you think he's going to do?" The worry in her voice stalled his response.

He didn't want her concerned about anything. She may appear strong to others, but Junior knew the truth. Sissy had never been strong, not as a child, and not as a young woman. Her sweet almost childlike nature caused many to think she was closer to fifteen than nineteen.

He pulled her into his arms, kissing her forehead. "I'm not ready to talk about it yet, sweetheart."

"I'm scared, Junior. Can you give me a hint?" She leaned into him, resting her head against his chest, wrapping her arms around his waist.

"What I will tell you is if Pa does what I imagine, it will be our opportunity to get away."

Pulling back, guileless eyes looked up at him. "Can we really leave them?" Moving one hand from his waist, she placed the open palm against her stomach.

"There's enough money for us to start our own life together. I don't want to continue robbing banks and stages, Sissy."

"What *do* you want, Junior?"

"For us to marry and start a family somewhere far away from Pa and Ma."

"Where would we go?"

"Somewhere in California, where we aren't known. I can get work on the docks of San Francisco, in a saloon, or on a ranch. There are many opportunities farther west, Sissy." He clasped her shoulders, squeezing. "It's our chance, sweetheart."

Pursing her lips, she rubbed her stomach.

"Are you sick?"

The question had Sissy lifting her head to study his features. Sincerity and concern were etched around his eyes and in the lines of his mouth. She thought of keeping the secret a little longer, dismissing the idea. It was time to tell him and face the consequences.

"I'm pregnant."

Whatever else Junior planned to say died on his lips as he stared down at what was a slightly rounded stomach. It took a moment before he locked on the frightened look in her eyes.

"You're certain?"

"Yes."

Instead of the irritation, or even denial, she expected, Junior picked her up, twirling her around. "You're having my baby."

A giggle escaped her lips. As he continued turning in a circle, the giggle turned into laughter before he set her down. Cupping her face in his hands, Junior kissed her, long and soundly before lifting his head.

"I love you, Sissy."

"I love you, too."

Taking her hand in his, he guided her to one of the two empty rooms at the back of the house. At early evening, the light had already faded. There were no curtains on the windows, nothing to stop those walking past from looking inside. One of the bedrooms would provide the most privacy he could find.

Cupping her face, his gaze settled on hers. "Does Ma know?"

"No one knows except the two of us, Junior."

Kissing her, he dropped his hands. "We have to get away before she or Pa begins to suspect. If they discover you're expecting a baby..." His voice trailed off, unable to say aloud the fear building in his chest.

"They won't let me keep it, Junior." Her voice quivered. "You know they won't."

Wrapping his arms around her, he pressed Sissy's head against his chest. "We won't give them the chance to do anything to you or the baby. No matter what Pa plans, you and I will be leaving Splendor very soon, sweetheart."

On Gabe's order, Hex, Zeke, and Hawke rode out well before dawn. Beau had come across an old wanted poster of a Jerome Taggert, the illustration and description matching Tim Jones. A note at the end mentioned him traveling with two others, suspected to be his brothers, Theo and Byron.

Hawke had nothing else to go on except what he'd learned from Hex and Zeke. It was enough. They wanted to bring Tim, and any companions, back to town alive. All believed they'd learn more about the shooting at the boardinghouse, as well as any connection the gunmen had with the other four at the table.

Leading the three, Hex's mind moved between the job ahead and Christina. No longer did he harbor any doubts how much he wanted her. A woman such as Alana would never be able to offer him what he craved.

Real love, devotion, and affection for a child not her own. He could imagine spending days and nights with her for the rest of their lives. Hex wanted another child and knew Christina craved a big family. She was a natural mother. Little ruffled her, a requirement when marrying a lawman.

Zeke had asked if he loved her. Hex hadn't thought much about his feelings for her other than he enjoyed their time together, missed Christina when apart. Did that mean he loved her?

At one time, he'd believed himself in love with Lucy's mother, Alice. He knew it now to be nothing more than affection and perhaps a good measure of lust. When he'd learned of her death and the existence of his daughter, there'd been a deep ache, not the crushing blow he would've expected.

Hex knew the loss of Christina would be devastating to him and Lucy. Did that turn his deep caring into love? All he had were questions with no specific answers.

At the fork in the trail he drew up, waiting for Zeke and Hawke to join him. One way had seen considerable travel, the other more of a deer path. "From here, it will take us about twenty minutes to reach their camp."

Zeke leaned over his saddlehorn, searching the wider of the two trails. "Assuming they haven't packed up and left. Jones may have recognized you from the boardinghouse, Hex."

"Maybe. I guess we'll find out once we find them."

"If we find them," Zeke muttered.

Hex shifted in his saddle, locking his gaze with his brother's. "Something eating at you?"

Scrubbing a hand down his face, Zeke shook his head. "Nothing I'm talking about."

Narrowing his eyes, Hex studied him. "Does this have anything to do with Francesca?"

"Hell no." The response was too quick and much too rigid, making both Hex's and Hawke's lips twitch. Hex would have to ask Zeke more about the female attorney later.

"Then let's get moving." Hex clucked to move his horse forward, ready to end this search and get back home.

Chapter Twenty

Jerome rode behind his brothers, peering over his shoulder every few minutes as they put more distance between them and their camp. He hadn't wanted to move until they'd collected their money and ridden from the Montana Territory. The appearance of four people he recognized changed their plans.

All had been at a table at the boardinghouse the night they'd fulfilled their agreement with the Grooms. Reason told him they could never identify them. He, Theo, and Byron had been wearing bandanas, so no one should be able to point to them as the killers. The fact they'd inadvertently discovered their camp changed his mind. Even though they hadn't recognized him, he couldn't take chances with his brothers.

Theo rested a hand on the cantle of his saddle, yelling over his shoulder. "Where are we headed, Jerome?"

"South around Splendor, then north. We'll camp up there until we get our money, which will be soon."

His patience with the Grooms had run out. They'd known the location of their camp, never bothering to bring the money. Jerome figured they felt protected in a town where people seemed to know everyone.

"How soon?" Byron called. Of the twins, he'd always been the most impatient. In this case, his desire to get their money was justified.

Jerome had heard about the competition and ranch rodeo, already deciding to use it to their advantage. Once settled in their new camp, he'd send his brothers to town to confirm the Grooms hadn't fled. He didn't believe they had.

Their camp had been located not far from the trail heading west out of Splendor. It was the only safe direction the Grooms could go. One of the Taggerts had scouted it each day since the shooting, confirming none of the family had been passengers.

The ruffling wind brought a sound Jerome hoped not to hear. Horses neighing and hoofs pounding the hard ground drew all their attention.

"Ride," Jerome hissed, kicking his horse.

Taking a trail heading farther south, they rode until coming out of the cover of the trees. Using hand motions, he signaled to split-up.

Last night, Jerome hoped they wouldn't have use for an alternate plan, but experience told him to be prepared. He knew the noises could've been anyone. His gut warned the horses they heard were coming for them.

Taking a glance behind him, Jerome spotted Theo backtracking in a wide arc, heading southwest instead of north. To his other side, he saw Byron ride east, as if heading to Big Pine, sweeping south into the cover of more trees.

Jerome rode due north, not taking the trail leading into the foothills. Instead, he guided his horse northeast, into a massive mixture of scrub, trees, and rock formations. Instead of wide expanses, he navigated his horse through slim openings between boulders, along deer trails, and up steep inclines.

It took almost an hour before the trail opened enough for him to rein around to view the valley below. His vantage point spanned for miles in a one-hundred-eighty degree arc. He saw nothing. No group of men on horseback or clouds of dust.

Jerome thought of Theo and Byron, praying they'd gotten away and would meet him tonight at the prearranged spot.

The echo of a shout caught his attention. He glanced down the hill, seeing a group of three men winding their way up the hill toward him. Reining around, he kicked the horse, riding across the open area to vanish within another dense thicket.

Compared to the first part of the hill, this part appeared almost impenetrable. Several times he had to back up a few yards in search of an easier trail. The climb took precious minutes he didn't have, the switchbacks at times putting him closer to those who followed than away from them.

He estimated an hour elapsed before he reached the summit, a mocking grin spreading across his face. The three men pursuing them had followed him, not Theo and Byron. His brothers had gotten away. If they did catch him, there'd be no evidence connecting the killing at the boardinghouse to him or his brothers.

The only people who could identify them were the Grooms. By exposing the Taggerts, they'd be admitting to hiring them to kill the U.S Marshal.

He'd done it. Drawn the riders away from Theo and Byron. The time had come to make camp and wait.

Removing his hat, Hex swiped a sleeve across his forehead, more from frustration than the temperature. Late March and the air was still cool, but the challenging climb in rough terrain shot their body heat up to an uncomfortable degree. That, and the fact their prey could have them in his sights at any point.

Stopping at the opening in the trail, Hex shifted to grab his canteen, taking a long swallow. Zeke and Hawke did the same while remaining vigilant. They were aware of the lack of evidence. Hex's instincts would go only so far before proof would be needed.

Their hope had been to question Jones and his partners. Finding the remains of their camp, Hawke had begun tracking. It hadn't taken long to find three sets of horse tracks heading in the same direction. Hex had been right, Jones wasn't alone.

Something had spooked them, causing the three to take several divergent trails. Hex had chosen to follow the man he recognized as Jones, letting the others go. His goal had changed to following him long enough to determine the location of the man's new camp.

Dax and two of Gabe's deputies, Dutch and Shane, rode into town, exhausted and hungry from the long ride from Wyoming. Their first stop was the jail. They waited a few minutes before Gabe arrived. After greetings, he motioned for them to sit down.

"I'll make this short," Dax said, before explaining the results of their journey. "We arrived at Fort Laramie soon after the rustlers had herded the cattle into the pens. While Dutch kept watch outside, Luke, Shane, and I pushed our way into the commander's office as the leader of the rustlers sat down across the desk. I'm certain the commander would've had us arrested if Shane hadn't been there. Before money could change hands, I stated our case. Shane's relationship with the commander helped a great deal."

"Plus, we'd fulfilled contracts at Fort Laramie in the past," Luke added. "The commander remembered us. He had his stock master check the brands. It took a while, but they arrested the rustler and his men."

"We were paid for the herd." Dax scrubbed a hand down his face. "Couldn't wait to get away from there."

"Anything to add, Shane?" Gabe asked.

"No, sir. I'm glad you ordered me to go along."

"Dutch?"

"Nothing different than what Shane said, Gabe. His past with the commander helped a great deal. I doubt we'll see those rustlers back in this area, or anywhere else."

"Have you boys eaten?"

"We're headed to the boardinghouse. Why don't you join us, Gabe?" Dax stood. "It's on Luke and me."

"I believe I will. It'll give us time to talk about the rodeo and competition, assuming it's still on for this Sunday." Standing, Gabe grabbed his hat, then adjusted his gunbelt.

Dax followed him to the door. "Nothing has changed. Besides, Rachel might shoot me if I tried to postpone it now." He and the other men chuckled as they headed outside.

The sun had begun its descent over the western mountains, the sky beginning to fade from deep blue to soft purples and pinks. Dax knew by the time they finished supper and left for the ranch, sunset would be over, the sky dark except for millions of bright stars and a three-quarter moon.

He was ready to get home to his wife and two boys. Dax didn't have to ask Luke if he felt the same.

Luke and Dax spent more time over supper than they expected, talking about the activities planned for Sunday while enjoying seconds on dessert and coffee. The rest of the Pelletier men had headed straight back to the ranch, or in Travis's case, went home to Isabella.

The two rode the trail in silence, their stomachs full, exhausted, and ready to get home. At a fork in the road, Dax reined up. To the left would take them to their ranch. He glanced right, focusing on what had caught his attention.

Off in the distance came the light from an almost imperceptible fire. If he'd blinked, he would've missed it. It could be anyone. Men from the nearby ranches or one of Baron Klaussner's hunting parties, although the location made no sense. He preferred hunting farther north or east.

Dax couldn't shake the feeling it might be one of the men Hex, Zeke, and Hawke had followed. They arrived back in Splendor as Luke and Dax were leaving. Their quick explanation of Jones had been meant as a warning.

They'd lost his trail. Even with Hex's instincts screaming he was involved in the murder, they had no proof. Not a single piece of information that he and the two who'd been with him were guilty of the crime.

"Is that a fire?" Luke moved farther along the trail east.

"Seems so. Could be anyone."

"But you don't believe that."

Dax shook his head, urging his horse forward. "No."

"We should check on it." Luke clucked, his palomino stallion, Prince, responding immediately.

"Wait. It's gone." Dax narrowed his gaze, continuing to stare at where he'd seen the light. He remembered the approximate location, but without the glow of the fire, they'd be riding in blind. They'd fought in too many battles during the war not to know it could be a trap.

"Let's wait a little longer to see if we spot it again."

They did, but after ten minutes, Dax decided to attempt a closer look. Luke followed, the men moving as silently as possible on the two well-trained horses.

The faint neighing of another horse stilled their movements. After several moments, they nudged their horses toward the sound. Muffled voices wafted through the air, causing them to stop again.

Glancing at each other, Dax motioned Luke to dismount. They'd be going closer on foot. Prince, and Dax's stallion, Hannibal, wouldn't go far. If the brothers needed them, a whistle would have the horses returning.

Grabbing their rifles, the two bent at the waist, taking careful steps as they sought those they knew to be up ahead. After hearing what they'd believed to be voices, the night grew silent. The fire of earlier didn't reappear.

The sharp crack of a rifle preceded a bullet whizzing between them. Without a word, they dropped to the ground, lifting their rifles.

"Did you see anything?" Luke asked.

"Muzzle flash to our right."

Rising to their knees, they shifted their rifles, securing them against their shoulders.

"One...two...three." Dax fired into the darkness an instant before Luke pulled the trigger. "Again," Dax ground out. Two more shots tore through the air. A string of curses was the only response. "We need to move. I'll go right."

Luke gave a terse nod, preparing to head left.

On Dax's signal, both rose from their knees, bending as low as possible. Before they could leave, another bullet whizzed through the air. All Dax heard was Luke's sharp intake of breath and muttered curse before he crumbled to the ground.

Chapter Twenty-One

Jerome dropped his rifle, running to tackle Byron. Coming up on top, he slugged his brother on the chin. "Are you a complete idiot? I said to scare them off, not kill them. Hell, we have enough problems without shooting one of the locals."

Standing, Jerome held out his hand to help his brother up. "You and Theo get back to the camp and stay there. I'll go see what damage you did."

Staying within the cover of the bush, he crouched, moving from one hiding place to another until no more than ten yards from where the man went down. "Where is he?" The whispered words tumbled from his lips as he scoured the area, finding nothing.

No body, no second rider, and no horses. Giving up his intention to hide, he circled the area over and over, checking everywhere a man could hide.

Five, ten, fifteen minutes passed without finding any trace. Jerome began to think he'd imagined the shooting, hadn't heard the man gasp. Placing fisted hands on his hips, he made one more circle before accepting whoever had taken the bullet had disappeared.

Dax glanced over his shoulder every few seconds, confirming Luke still clung to Prince's saddle. Blood soaked his shirt, dripping to the ground as they made their way to town.

The shot had clipped him on the left shoulder. Dax didn't believe it had done much damage, but you didn't ignore a bullet wound, no matter how benign it appeared.

Reaching the edge of town, Dax increased his pace, Prince following. They'd gone no more than fifty yards before Dutch ran toward them.

"Who did this, Dax?"

"I don't know, but he needs to get to the clinic."

"I'll let Doc McCord know." Dutch ran ahead, bursting through the clinic door. By the time Dax and Luke arrived, Clay and Georgina Wise, a nurse who'd arrived in town with Francesca, were ready.

Ignoring Luke's weak protests, Dutch and Dax each supported one side as they helped him up the steps and inside.

Clay held open the door to one room. "In here."

Luke scowled at Dax and Dutch. "It's a scratch, Doc. Fix me up and let me get home."

A cursory glance at the mangled flesh told Clay it was a little more than a scratch. "How about you let me make the decision on how bad it is. Nurse Wise, please clean the wound for Mr. Pelletier while I speak with his brother."

"Yes, doctor." She didn't spare a glance at the other men before dipping a clean cloth in warm water.

A moment before the door to the examination room closed, Georgina allowed herself a brief look at the one man to catch her attention since arriving in Splendor. Dutch McFarlin had never shown the slightest interest in her. Then again, no man ever did.

Finishing, she picked up the bowl and cloth, setting them aside before locating the bottle of whiskey in the cupboard. "I'll get the doctor."

"Wait." Luke tried to lever himself up on one arm, the effort causing him to fall back.

"What are you doing?"

Grimacing, he reached out his hand, taking the bottle from her. "I need a drink before you waste good whiskey on a wound that doesn't need it."

Suppressing a grin, she supported his head, allowing Luke several swallows before pulling the bottle away. "That's enough, Mr. Pelletier. Are you ready now?"

Eyes a little glassy, he nodded. "Get it over with."

"I'll get Doctor McCord." Opening the door, she jerked to a stop. Dutch stood on the other side, resting his back against the wall while Dax and Clay talked on the other side of the room.

"Oh, Deputy McFarlin."

Straightening, he stared at her a moment, brows scrunched in concentration. "You're Miss Wise."

It took three tries to swallow the lump in her throat. Taking a step away from him, she clasped her hands together, tongue darting out to moisten her lips. "Yes. I'm one of the nurses. I came to town with Miss O'Reilly and the other women."

Dutch's lips twitched at the way her face flushed. "I know."

"You do?" Her shocked expression surprised him.

"I try to welcome all beautiful women to town, Miss Wise."

Heat crept up her neck to her face at the same time her jaw dropped. *Does he really think I'm beautiful?* Searching for a response, relief washed over her when the front door opened.

"Where is my husband?" The words were out before Ginny Pelletier made it into the clinic. "Is he all right?" Rachel appeared right behind her, hurrying to Dax.

"He's going to be fine, Ginny," Clay responded. "I need to tend to the wound. Is he ready, Nurse Wise?"

Clearing her throat, she did her best to compose herself before answering. "Yes, doctor. Excuse me, Deputy McFarlin."

"Dutch."

"Wha...what?"

"Call me Dutch."

Lips parting, she snapped them shut before giving a terse nod and following the doctor and Ginny into the exam room.

Dax took Rachel's hand, encouraging her to sit down. "It won't take long. Luke isn't going to want to stay here any longer than needed."

As she lowered herself into the chair, the door burst open. Hex, followed by Zeke and Hawke, stalked into the clinic and approached Dutch.

"We heard Luke was shot."

"Doc McCord is tending to him now, Hex. He and Dax were on their way to the ranch when they spotted something."

Dax joined them. "We spotted the light of a fire and went to check it out. Whoever was there saw us and shot Luke."

"More than one person?" Hex asked.

"It was too dark to be certain, but I believe there were two, maybe three by the number of horses we heard. Do you know who they are?"

Hex removed his hat, threading fingers through his hair. "Could be the same men who shot Henry Steed in the boardinghouse. We tried going after them, but they split up and got away. Let me know where this happened, Dax, and we'll head out at first light tomorrow."

As Dax described the location to them, Hex thought of Christina, how much he missed her, wanted to wrap her in his arms and never let go. The thought didn't surprise him. She hadn't been far from his mind all day.

"I need to speak with Gabe. Then I'm going to eat and get some sleep." The last two with Christina.

Hex could smell the food before opening the door to Christina's house. Stepping inside, he'd made it a couple feet before Lucy ran out of Cici's bedroom, flinging herself into his arms for him to twirl her around.

"Papa. Where have you been?" She touched his cheek with her palm.

Setting her on the floor, his gaze connected with Christina's. She stood at the sink, mashing what he presumed to be potatoes.

"We waited for you. Have you had supper?"

He smiled at Cici when she emerged from her bedroom, then walked to stand behind Christina. It took all his control not to slip his arms around her, rest his chin on her head as he drew her against him. Instead, he leaned over her shoulder, lifting the lid off the often used iron pot.

"Smells wonderful." He dipped his hand inside, removing a chunk of beef, popping it into his mouth.

"Hey." She softly tapped his hand.

"I'm just making certain it's up to your usual standards." He smacked his lips together. "It is."

Laughing, Christina finished the potatoes. "I'm glad you approve. Lucy, Cici, please set the table. I'll fill the plates."

Minutes later, the four sat around her dining table, finishing a prayer. Lucy gave this one, ending with thanks for bringing her father home safe. The words caused a lump to form in Hex's chest. He still had a hard time believing the ray of sunshine next to him was his daughter. As always, the pang of joy brought an equally strong bite of regret, wishing he'd known about her sooner.

"Did you find Mr. Jones?"

Hex shook his head, swallowing a mouthful of succulent beef. "They were gone when we reached their camp. We may have found where they are now. We'll leave again tomorrow morning." He glanced at the girls, realizing what he was asking. "Are you—"

She held up a hand, interrupting him. "Don't worry. Lucy will be fine with Cici and me."

"We get out of school early tomorrow, Papa." She shoved more potatoes into her mouth, eyes bright. "Christina is going to let us help her make a pie and finish our dolls."

"Dolls?"

"You remember, Papa. We've been sewing dolls for weeks."

Christina snickered but didn't correct her. It had been less than a week since they'd started, making forms, and stuffing them before sewing clothes. They still needed to add hair and finish the faces.

"The girls are doing an excellent job. When they finish their dolls, I'll teach them how to make a simple apron."

"Christina is going to let us pick out the fabric, Papa. I want red."

Finishing his meal, Hex slid the plate a few inches away. "What about you, Cici?"

"Yellow. It was Millie's favorite color." The young girl's mention of her late sister quieted the table for several long minutes. Christina broke the silence.

"I remember one yellow dress she bought to attend a soiree. Our stepmother didn't like it, but Millie insisted on wearing it. She was by far the most beautiful girl at the party."

The story returned a smile to Cici's face. "She's better now, isn't she, Chrissy?"

"Yes, she is. No pain and surrounded by...love." Christina's voice hitched on the last. She would always miss her twin sister.

"How about we take a ride on Saturday after visiting Millie's grave?"

Christina fought to stop the burn of tears at the back of her eyes, refusing to let them fall. "That would be lovely, Hex."

"Can we have another picnic, Papa?"

"We sure can, button."

Lucy giggled. She loved it when he called her by the nickname her gramma gave her.

"We don't have to order from Suzanne. I'd be happy to pack fried chicken, biscuits, jam, and pie."

"You're already doing so much for us, Chrissy."

A warm smile curved her lips. "I love all of it, Hex. You have your work and I have mine."

Leaning back in his chair, a grin appeared. "All right. Do you ladies prefer wagon or horses this time?"

"Horses, Papa!"

Cici and Christina agreed, all of them feeling the excitement of a day away from town.

Glancing around the table, Hex couldn't stop the tightening in his chest. This could be his family. All he needed was time with Christina and the courage to admit his feelings.

Chapter Twenty-Two

Junior stood rigid at the door of their hotel room on Friday afternoon, peeking into the hall. "What's taking you so long to pack, Sissy?"

Hands trembling, she hurriedly stuffed items into her satchel, heart hammering at what Junior intended. "I thought we were leaving Sunday."

Checking the hall once more, he shot an impatient look at her. "Not any longer. I don't trust Pa to change his plans. We have to be a long way from here before he wakes up tomorrow."

Without thought, she splayed a hand over her stomach. "When will we leave?"

"Tonight, after Pa and Ma go to bed. We'll take horses from the livery." Closing the door, he walked to the wardrobe, removing his satchel. Setting it on the bed, he withdrew a pair of pants and shirt, tossing them down.

"You'll need to wear these tonight. They'll make it easier for you to ride. We're also changing our names. No more Junior or Sissy."

"I already have a name. The one my parents gave me."

Walking around the bed, he put a comforting arm around her. "You can't use it, sweetheart." Reaching into a pocket, he handed her a piece of paper. "These are our new names."

Unfolding the paper, she read his familiar script, the first sign of a smile curving her mouth. "Anna and William McAllister. I like them. Do I get to call you Willie?"

He threw back his head and laughed. "William, Will, or Willie. Whatever you want."

Kissing her cheek, he dropped his arm to kneel by the bed. Slipping his hand under the mattress, he pulled out a closed leather pouch, holding it in the air.

"This is all we have, but it should be enough to get us to California. This is the perfect time to leave. The weather is getting better and much of the snow will have melted. That's why we're heading south, then west."

"You know I'm not a strong rider."

"You'll do fine. I won't let anything happen to you or the baby. There's no reason anyone should follow us, which means we can go at an easier pace. We'll change to riding a stagecoach as soon as we can."

Nodding, she continued to rub her stomach. "Pa's going to be mad as a hungry hog when he learns we've left. Won't he try to follow us?"

"He has big plans for Sunday. Afterward, he might try to find us, but I doubt it. Besides, we'll be long gone by then."

Giving a slow nod, she squared her shoulders. "What do you want me to do?"

Pride swelled at her courage. "We'll have supper with Pa and Ma tonight. Afterward, you and I will take a walk, as we always do. Nothing changes, except when we return to our room, we'll wait for midnight."

"Then leave?"

"Yes." Wrapping his arms around her waist, he lowered his head, kissing her until he sensed her calm. "This is for the best, sweetheart. We have to get away from my parents before they realize you're pregnant. I don't know what they'll do if they find out."

"I know what will happen. They'll do something so the baby is never born. If that doesn't succeed, they'll give it away. I won't let anything happen to our child." Her voice rose, becoming more agitated with each sentence. Burying her face in his chest, she clutched his arms.

He bent next to her ear. "That's why we must leave tonight. The longer we stay, the more chance Ma will get suspicious."

Junior wondered why his parents had insisted he and Sissy share a bed since they'd taken her in. As they got older, he kept expecting Ma to separate them. He didn't believe Pa cared what happened between them, but Ma would.

Junior felt certain they knew he and Sissy had been intimate for a long time, yet they'd done nothing to stop it. They had a strange sense of family. There were times he even wondered if he was their son. Or, if like Sissy, they'd taken him in at a young age.

He often found himself hoping there wasn't a drop of Groom blood in his veins. Over the years, he'd come to hate being connected to those who claimed to be his parents.

Junior detested how Pa had hired gunmen to kill the man suspected of being a U.S. Marshal. There'd been no proof, yet Pa refused to believe the man an innocent.

Worse, the men who'd killed him were still out there, waiting for payment.

"How much longer before we have supper, William?"

He grinned at the use of his new name. "An hour, Anna. How are you feeling?"

"Good, but tired."

"You should nap. I'll wake you in time to get ready."

She stretched out, catching his hand in hers. "I love you, Willie."

His gaze wandered over her, settling on her soft, green eyes. Brushing a kiss across her lips, he felt his chest squeeze. "And I love you, Anna."

"We have to get out of here, Jerome." Theo dropped his smoke onto the ground, grinding it out with the heel of his boot. "You know they're going to come after us. The money isn't worth going to jail or dying."

Jerome stared at the ground, anger still simmering at what Byron had done. There'd been no need to shoot the stranger. If they'd continued to hide and stayed quiet, the men would've ridden away. Instead, they'd broken camp, riding deep into the rugged terrain northeast. He raised his head to meet his brother's steady scowl.

"You're right, Theo. The money isn't worth it. Still, those men didn't see who shot at them, and I hate leaving knowing that old man stole from us."

Theo tossed a stick onto the small fire, now emitting just enough heat to lessen the chill. "We'd have to ride into town to confront him and get what's owed us. I'm not anxious for anyone to tie us to the Grooms."

Byron stretched out his long legs, watching the thin plume of smoke rise several feet before disappearing. "I agree with Theo. The sheriff and his men are going to be watching for us. They may not know we're the ones who shot the lawman, but they'll be watching anyone who's new to town. Let's pack up and get the hell out of here."

Scrubbing a hand down his face, Jerome pursed his lips. He had an idea, one he hadn't shared with either brother. "I know how we can get our money back."

Two sets of eyes locked onto his, Byron being the one to respond first. "When were you planning to share it with us?"

"I've got some more thinking to do on it. I can't be seen in town, but one of you can ride in, discover what I need to know, and report back to me."

"Tell me what you need and I'll leave in the morning," Theo said.

Byron shook his head. "I should be the one to go. It was me who shot the man and got us into this trouble."

"It could've been me," Theo protested. "I was ready to shoot, but you pulled the trigger first."

The exchange continued another minute, the twins making arguments why they should be the one to go before Jerome interrupted.

"Enough." Pushing up, he stalked across the camp to an opening between the rocks. Though several miles away, the moonlight gave him an unobstructed view to Splendor. A few lights still shown in the distance, but it was too far to hear the music and shouts coming from the saloons.

He didn't want to send either brother to town. Putting them in danger gave him no pleasure. It was his job to learn what he needed to make a decision—go after Groom or leave the territory.

Pressing the palms of his hands into his eyes, he let out a slow breath in an attempt to clear his head. Nothing had gone as he'd expected since arriving in Splendor.

He'd met Groom in a small town in the eastern side of Montana. They'd talked several times, the elder man pointing out the U.S. Marshal who'd been following them. He'd taken Groom's word Henry Steed was a lawman. Jerome now wondered if it was the truth. It didn't matter. Steed was dead and Groom owed them money.

Decision made, he returned to where Theo and Byron waited. "I'll be the one going."

Byron jumped up, hands fisted at his sides. "You can't. Someone may recognize you."

"I won't put either one of you in danger."

Theo stood, joining Byron. "You were fine with the decision ten minutes ago."

"Changed my mind. I'll leave at first light. You two will stay here, be ready when I return so we can figure out what to do next."

Theo rubbed the back of his neck. "I don't like it, Jerome."

"Neither do I." Byron bent down, picking up a thin stick to toss on the fire. "Why don't we all go?"

Jerome's expression turned fierce. "No. You and Theo will stay here and wait for me. If I'm not back by nightfall, clear the camp and leave. Head to Salt Lake City and wait one week. If I don't arrive by then, you're on your own."

Byron's jaw clenched. "This isn't what was decided when we first headed out. No matter what, we stick together. If you take off, I'm going to follow."

"Same with me, Jerome. You can't force us to stay in camp."

His response was a series of curses as he paced around the camp. Theo and Byron were right. He couldn't stop his brothers from following, which meant they would ride together.

Hex finished the last bite of chicken, following it with a long swallow of coffee before pushing his plate away. Christina and the girls had already eaten, and she'd put Lucy and Cici to bed. Right now, she was delivering a plate of dessert to Isabella and her husband, Travis.

Taking his plate to the sink, he washed it quickly, pouring himself another cup of coffee. The dried apple pie called to him. He placed a large slice on a plate, taking it and the coffee back to the table.

He, Zeke, and Hawke had been on the trail all day without finding a trace of the gunmen. The deputies were certain whoever shot Luke had also killed Henry Steed.

When they'd returned tonight, Gabe had given them even worse news. Henry Steed was no normal citizen. He was U.S. Marshal Michael Mulvaney, considered one of the finest lawmen west of the Mississippi.

After the rodeo and competition on Sunday, Gabe would be sending two groups of deputies out to find those responsible. He wanted them returned to Splendor, dead or alive, it didn't matter as long as they found the men who'd killed Mulvaney and shot Luke.

Hex had made the difficult decision to cancel their picnic on Saturday, choosing to keep the girls close to town. Instead, they'd be attending the ranch rodeo at the Pelletier ranch. He'd also agreed to be part of the shooting team composed of deputies.

Chewing a large piece of pie, he couldn't ignore a pang of concern niggling at him. Gabe requested a few deputies to stay in town during the rodeo. Dutch, Beau, Cash, and Shane volunteered, all excellent. The knowledge should've relieved Hex's worries. It didn't.

The Grooms were still in town. He didn't trust them, thought they were more involved in the shooting of the U.S. Marshal than they wanted anyone to believe. Then there were the men who'd actually killed Mulvaney. Executed was a more accurate term.

He thought of that night, the way the other four at the table had leaned away from Mulvaney when the shooters entered. Not when the bullets began to fly, but before, as if they knew what to expect.

Hex also couldn't understand why the Grooms had stayed in Splendor. Gabe had warned them not to leave, having no actual authority to enforce it. In truth, they could've ignored his order at any time.

What made them stay? The question haunted him. Although a former bounty hunter, Hawke had doubts the Grooms were the people he'd been tracking, he'd kept an open mind. Hex had seen him follow the four around town on several occasions. He knew Hawke wanted to question them, but Gabe didn't believe they had enough to bring them to the jail.

Hex had begun thinking the opposite. Between the Grooms and Mulvaney's killers, something was very wrong in Splendor. He just needed to identify what.

Chapter Twenty-Three

Christina approached the back door of her house, anxious to visit with Hex. By now, he would've finished supper, probably eaten at least one piece of pie.

Opening the door, she stepped inside, surprised not to see Hex at the dining room table. Quietly treading through the kitchen, she came to an abrupt stop. Stretched out on her sofa was Hex, legs falling off the end, arms crossed over his chest, eyes closed.

Taking a few small steps, she got close enough to hear his soft snores. Christina stared at him for several long minutes, marveling at his relaxed features, the lines of worry smooth during sleep. As long as they'd known each other, she'd never seen him so at peace. At rest, he appeared to be a boy rather than a grown man.

Reluctantly, she moved away. Going to her bedroom, she selected a blanket from one of her trunks, shaking it out. It was a quilt she and Millie had sewn together years before. Her favorite.

Returning to the living room, she placed it over Hex, tucking it around him. He let out a deep breath, but didn't stir. Extinguishing the lamp, she backed away, satisfied with her decision not to wake him.

Before retiring, she peeked in on the girls. Not surprising, they were huddled next to each other, sound asleep. Christina took one more look at Hex before entering her bedroom, closing the door on a quiet click.

Lowering herself onto the bed, she allowed herself a smile. Hex had been comfortable enough to fall asleep in her house when he could've walked the short distance to his place. He'd *wanted* to stay, even if it meant sleeping on an uncomfortable sofa, too short for his long frame.

Without undressing, she fell back on the bed, pulling the cover over her. Christina closed her eyes, a faint grin curling her lips. Within minutes, she was softly snoring, the same as Hex.

They moved in the shadows of the darkening night, Junior keeping a tight hold on Sissy's hand. The two had left later than intended, waiting longer than expected for Pa and Ma to retire for the night.

He'd already hidden their satchels in the bushes behind the livery's corral, waiting a few hours after Noah left. The horses were saddled and ready, food stuffed into saddlebags. He'd secure the satchels behind the saddles, then they'd be off.

A deep cough had Junior shoving her behind him. "Don't make a sound."

Lips trembling, she gave a shaky nod as her hand covered her stomach. It had become instinctive to cover their unborn child when anxious. Sensing someone approaching, she closed her eyes, praying they weren't spotted. A moment later, Junior's hand tightened on hers.

"It's safe now." Tugging her behind him, he continued behind the buildings to the end of the street and stopped. "We need to pass Chinatown to reach the livery. You must stay with me and keep quiet. Are you ready?"

"Yes." The whispered word held steely determination. "I'm ready."

At this late hour, and except for a few people staggering out of the saloons, the streets were deserted. Junior knew there were at least two deputies patrolling the streets, but he'd yet to see them.

"Let's go." Leading the way, he ran at a slow pace so Sissy could keep up. It took less than two minutes to reach the corral of the livery, where he retrieved their satchels.

Sissy kept her gaze moving around them, seeing nothing of concern. "What now?"

He tossed both satchels over the fence, hearing two thumps when they hit the ground. "I'll scale the fence, secure our belongings, cut off the lock, and open the gate. We'll mount up inside the livery, then head out. Will you be all right for a few minutes?"

"I'll be fine, Junior. Please do what you need to so we can leave."

Brushing a quick kiss across her lips, he climbed over the fence, dropping to the ground and stilled. The horses danced around, making slight noises. Nothing to warn others of their intentions.

Several minutes later, she heard the sound of breaking metal before the gate opened, Junior motioning her to join him. She adjusted the large pants, closed the bulky coat around her, and shoved her boot into the stirrup. Using all her strength, Sissy bounced a couple times before swinging into the saddle with a satisfied thump.

"I'm ready."

Junior clucked, moving his horse out of the livery, Sissy following close behind. Once outside the livery, he reined the horse around, closing the gate. He'd left money in an envelope, securing it to the back door of the blacksmith shop, hoping it would cover what they'd taken.

Circling behind the corral, he guided his horse south, keeping the pace slow so as not to draw attention from anyone who might still be awake. Or worse, the deputies he knew were out there.

Time crept along before reaching the far end of town and the trail away from Splendor. Turning the corner to cross Rimrock Street, Junior reined to a stop, putting a finger to his lips.

Up ahead, one of the deputies came to a halt at the end of Frontier Street, taking a look around before crossing to the St. James Hotel to head in the other direction.

Junior waited several minutes before clucking again. Reversing their path, he ignored the trail, intending to make a broad arc around Splendor. A sharp shout behind them had both glancing over their shoulders. A second deputy they hadn't noticed ran toward them from the direction of the livery. The unlocked gate to the livery corral must've blown open, alerting the deputy.

Another shout triggered Junior to kick his horse. "We have to get out of here, Sissy."

A shot rang through the night. Even with the money he'd left, horse stealing was a serious crime, often ending in hanging. Another shout was followed by two more shots, both whizzing past them.

Guiding the horses back to the trail west, Junior's heart raced. He knew Sissy would be scared, fear beginning to guide her actions. She'd also do all in her power to stay close to him and protect their unborn child. They weren't prepared to lose a posse tracking them. Junior knew he might get away, but they'd need a miracle with Sissy.

Clouds closed over the moon, making it harder for a posse to follow, but also more difficult for them to find their way through the thick vegetation. Two hours outside of Splendor, Junior slowed, guiding the horses well off the trail into a thick copse of trees. Sliding to the ground, he hurried to Sissy, holding his arms up.

"How do you feel?" His worried gaze studied her as he set her down beside him.

Shoving up the long sleeves of her coat, she swiped strands of hair from her face. "Tired, but I'm fine." Sissy nervously glanced around, listening for anyone who may be following them. "Do you think they're still out there?"

"I don't know. We won't stay here long, just enough for the horses and us to rest. We have a long way to go before making camp." Drawing her to him, he wrapped his arms around her, trying to absorb the fear he saw in her features. "Are you hungry?"

"No, but I could use some water."

Releasing her, he grabbed her canteen. "Here. Not too much. We have to make it last until we find a lake or stream."

Taking it, she took three shallow swallows before handing the canteen back. When he went to put it away, she grabbed his arm.

"You have to drink some, Junior."

He held her gaze a moment before taking a couple gulps. "We should be on our way in a few minutes. There are bushes over there. Take care of what you need, then we'll leave. Don't go too far, Sissy."

Junior waited until she'd disappeared behind a nearby bush before taking care of his own needs. He heard nothing, making him wonder if they'd found the money he'd left at the livery and abandoned the search. Chuckling at the absurd thought, he waited by the horses, watching Sissy emerge from the shadows.

Mounting, he guided them out using another trail. Emerging into an open meadow, he motioned for them to increase their pace, galloping across the area toward the cover of trees.

Using the stars as a guide, he continued south, then west, hoping it would take them to Boise. His original plan was to cut through Wyoming to Salt Lake City, then take the railroad to San Francisco. The last few days in Splendor, he'd heard about the Shoshone, Arapahoe, and Cheyenne, all present in Wyoming. From what he learned, Junior had no desire to confront them.

With the snow rapidly melting, Boise would be a better option. He knew nothing of the Indians in the Idaho Territory, and could only hope they weren't as hostile as those in Wyoming. From Boise, they could still go south, ending up in Utah.

Approaching an opening in the lush cover of the forest, they continued for close to a mile over open ground. The views in the predawn light were stunning, the deep green of emerging spring spectacular. Sissy removed her hat, allowing her long strawberry blonde hair to fall around her shoulders. It felt good. Settling the hat back on her head, she sighed.

After allowing the horses to graze, they crossed the last hundred yards of the clearing. As they rode, he made plans to camp in the first secluded spot they came across.

"Junior?" The quiver in Sissy's voice had him reining up. The stark terror on her face caused his focus to shoot behind them to the wide open trail. Two men, about a mile back, rode in their direction.

"Come on." Kicking his horse, he led a path into the woods, taking a twisting path into the mountains.

Changing their course several times, it wasn't long before snow covered everything around them, making it easier for trackers to follow. Junior knew the temperature would continue to drop the higher up the mountain they rode. With the sun rising over the eastern hills, they were too exposed, more so in another hour. They needed to find a place to hide.

"Junior. Up there."

He whirled around to see where Sissy pointed. A tall grouping of boulders blocked the path not twenty yards away.

"Let's take a look."

It turned out to be much better than they could've imagined. They'd expected to hide behind the rocks. What they found was a shock.

The formation spread at least twenty yards wide and ten yards high. Its appearance reminded him of a fortress in the old stories, the perfect place to defend a medieval village. What he saw stilled his breath.

On the far side, the boulders merged into a hillside. A grouping of large, snow-covered bushes hid the entrance of a cave. "Stay here while I look inside."

He hurried back out five minutes later, grabbing his horse's reins. "Bring your horse and follow me." Junior held back the bushes, allowing her to enter the cave.

"Move as far inside as possible. Watch your step, as there are roots and small rocks cluttering the ground."

Following her inside, Junior handed Sissy his reins, returning to the opening to rearrange the bushes to cover their hiding place.

Sissy looked around, seeing little in the almost complete darkness. The longer she stood, the more her eyes adjusted. The rock ceiling appeared to be about eight feet high, plenty tall enough for the horses. The inside walls were irregular, giving them what she guessed to be a space with a ten foot diameter.

Ignoring the way her stomach growled, she forced herself to stay put. What she wanted to do was drop to the ground and sleep. Junior joined her a few minutes later, adjusting the bushes from the inside.

"If the men are still behind us, they'll have to locate the trail we took up the mountain. Then they'd have to go far enough to find the boulders and decide to ride around them. If we're lucky and can keep the horses quiet, we may make it through this."

Walking the horses as far back into the cave as possible, he dug into the saddlebags. They didn't have much of a choice. Cold chicken, beef jerky, wrapped biscuits, jam, and fruit bars. Thanks to the large tip he'd given the server at the boardinghouse, there was enough to get them through several days.

Grabbing a blanket, he spread it out, setting out the food before taking Sissy's hand. Seconds later, they sat down with their bounty between them.

Eating in silence, they stared around their temporary home, and waited.

Chapter Twenty-Four

"You sure they rode up this way, Grover?" Earl Keith retrieved a tin of chewing tobacco from his pocket, putting a generous portion in his mouth.

"Saw them myself. I thought it was two men. Then I saw the long blonde hair of one of them. I'm telling you they took this trail up the mountain, Earl."

"Seems like a waste of time. We don't know if they have anything we want. I'm thinking we should ride on to Boise or head south. There are good pickins' in both places."

Grover darted a look at his partner, snorting. "I ain't looking for none of their money. I want the girl. It's been a long time, and I'm sick of paying for it."

"You don't know nothing about that woman."

"What's there to know? We kill her companion and take what we want."

Earl snorted in disgust. "Could be he's her husband, Grover. He's not going to let us just take her."

"That's why we're going to kill him. If you ain't interested, you can watch."

"Hell. I thought we were going to tie 'em up, rob 'em, and ride out." Earl leaned away from his horse, spitting onto the trail. "What are we going to do with the woman once we're done with her?"

Scoffing, Grover continued up the trail. "Kill her."

Splendor

"Are you sure you don't want us to go after them, Noah?" Gabe leaned a hip against the edge of his desk, his friend since childhood rubbing the stubble on his jaw. He'd been rousted from sleep a little before sunup, not long after Dutch and Beau returned from following the thieves.

Stretching out his legs, Noah threaded his fingers in his lap. "Whoever took the horses left an envelope full of cash."

"Enough to cover what they took?"

"Real close, Gabe. Have you found out who they are?"

"Two men is what Dutch saw. He said one appeared to be a good bit smaller than the other. A satchel was secured to each saddle."

"Dutch told me he shouted at them, but they rode off." Noah rubbed his hands down his pants, shaking his head. "Let it go, Gabe. They must've been running away from someone."

"Are you sure you want to call off the posse?"

"Yes. Dutch and Beau lost the trail an hour out of town. I'm sure they could pick it up in daylight, but the money they left satisfies me. Wish I knew who they were."

"We're going to talk with people in town after breakfast. If we don't learn who they are, we'll speak to those with ranches nearby. I doubt they would've ridden in to steal horses from one of the distant ranches. This had to have been planned. If Dutch hadn't noticed the gate swinging open, we wouldn't have learned about it until you arrived this morning."

Shoving to his feet, Noah clasped Gabe on the shoulder. "Let me know if you find out who they are. I'll send up a prayer the life ahead of them is better than the one they rode away from."

Grover spotted the large rock formation first, noticed the horse tracks, and motioned for Earl to follow. They rode around one side. Other than the tracks, they saw nothing indicating the two were hiding.

Grover continued to search for any sign of them, a smile peeling across his face when he spotted several horse tracks next to a bush at the far side of the boulders. Reining his horse around, he led them several yards away, dismounting. Earl did the same.

"Looks like there's a cave behind those bushes." Drawing his six-shooter, Grover carefully made his way to the cave, Earl right behind him, gun in hand.

Stopping next to the bushes, the two planted their boots on the frozen ground, pointing their weapons straight ahead.

"Did you hear that?" Sissy sat up, then stood, gaze darting around to settle on the entrance to the cave.

Junior stood, hearing footfalls before they stopped. Grabbing his gun, he turned toward Sissy, lowering his voice to a whisper. "Get as far back as you can."

Gritting her teeth, she shook her head. "No. I'm staying with you."

"Do as I say, Sissy," he hissed, keeping his voice low.

Chin lifting, features set, she marched to her horse, pulling the revolver from the saddlebag. "If they've found us, two guns are better than one."

Sweat beaded on his forehead at the thought of Sissy and their baby being shot. He glanced at the back of the cave. It was, at most, fifteen feet deep, still within range of a revolver.

Moving to one side of the opening, he motioned for her to position herself opposite him. Junior put a finger to his lips. He didn't have to tell her to shoot to kill. At this range, they could hardly miss. Raising his gun in front of him, a small grin lifted the corners of his mouth when she did the same.

"Whoever's in there, come out. We ain't gonna hurt you." The voice was deep, raspy, and menacing.

Junior shook his head, keeping his gun raised.

"We know there are two of you in there. Show yourselves. I'll give you to the count of..."

Junior looked at Sissy, mouthing, "*I love you.*" She did the same, eyes glittering.

"One...two...three...four...five." Two shots whizzed into the cave, missing both of them, but grazed the flank of one horse. It bucked and whined, eyes wide with panic.

Cursing, he took determined steps backward, making soothing noises as he grabbed the reins. He pulled the horse to the far side of the cave, seeing Sissy do the same when another shot rang through the cave, this one missing both horses.

The same voice followed the gunshot. "We'll kill you and the horses if needed. It'd be best for you to come out."

They braced for another shot, but nothing happened. The sound of the brush being shoved aside had them stiffening. Moving so their backs were against the sides of the cave, they aimed their guns at the entrance to the cave.

"We ain't joking with ya." There were no other warnings.

Both men rushed forward, firing straight ahead, then stopped. Blinking, they waited for their eyes to adjust. The decision turned lethal.

Junior placed two shots into the chest of the man closest to him. The satisfaction he expected didn't come. As the man collapsed to the ground, Sissy shot at the second man, clipping his arm. She froze when he turned toward her, raising his gun, his face twisted in rage.

"You—"

A shot to his chest cut off whatever else he meant to say. Another shot, this one piercing his leg, had him screaming, dropping his gun to grab for his leg.

Growling, he stumbled toward Sissy, eyes feral as he attempted to reach her. Her hands shook when she tried to get a shot off. A second before he got to her, a bullet sliced through his neck, silencing him as he dropped to the ground.

He laid there, body twitching, blood soaking through his clothes, dripping from his mouth. Hands reaching out, he clutched at his neck. His attempts to stop the bleeding lasted moments before a final breath whooshed between his lips. He stilled for the final time.

She stared at the two dead men, body shuddering, her gun hanging loose in her fingers.

"Sissy, are you all right?" Junior's hands grasped her shoulders, turning her to face him. Her lips were trembling, eyes glassy and hooded, not meeting his. "Sissy. Look at me."

As if in pain, she lifted her head, face pale. "They're dead."

"Yes, they are. Those men meant to kill us." He glanced over his shoulder at the two men, his own stomach churning at the blood. "You did real well, sweetheart." Tugging her into his arms, he crushed her to him. "Are you going to be able to help us get ready to leave?"

She shifted away, nodding. "Yes. Just tell me what to do."

Rubbing his hands up and down her arms, he lowered his head, kissing her. "Can you tend to the injured horse? Clean the wound with water, then apply salve before leading both outside. I'll take care of the men and carry out anything we need to take."

"What about their horses?" Her color had begun to return, eyes more alert.

"We'll go through their belongings. We can sell what we can't use in Boise."

She did as he asked, talking in a soothing voice as she cleaned the blood from the horse's flank. Applying salve, she smoothed it along the wound, wiping the excess down her pants. Picking up the reins of both horses, she led them outside.

The soft breeze felt good. She took several large gulps of air, clearing her head while attempting to erase the images of the two men. The thought had her looking around. Their horses were several yards away, watching her without moving.

She marveled at the amount of supplies secured to their saddles. As she studied the items, Junior emerged from the cave, carrying extra guns. He said nothing as he stuffed them into their saddlebags.

"Their horses are over there."

Junior turned toward where Sissy nodded, closing the distance to study what the men carried with them.

Sorting through the supplies, he removed what they could use, leaving the rest before releasing the saddles.

Handing what they'd be keeping to Sissy, he carried the saddles into the cave, dropping them by the bodies. He didn't recognize either man, wondered why they'd made the fatal decision to follow him and Sissy. Without a doubt, he knew they weren't from Splendor.

As he left the cave, adjusting the bush to cover the entrance, he began to relax. There'd been no sign of the deputies since first leaving Splendor.

"Are you ready to go, Sissy?" He knew she was tired, but they had to keep moving. Even without being chased, there could still be men out there who saw them as an easy target. "Tuck your hair under the hat. We don't want to advertise you're a woman."

She hurried to do as he asked and mounted. "I'm ready."

Walking toward her with the two extra horses, he handed her one set of reins. "Are you going to be able to ride with an additional horse?"

Straightening and settling into the saddle, she glanced between the two horses, lifting her chin. "I can handle them, Junior."

Lips twitching, he mounted. "All right. Let's get moving."

Chapter Twenty-Five

"Where the hell are they? When I find that boy..." Pa's voice trailed off, his face twisted in rage. He suspected what Junior had done, but refused to accept it.

Ma clasped her hands together, face serene in an attempt to pacify his anger. "They didn't join us for breakfast and they aren't in their room. It means nothing, Pa. Why don't we take a stroll around town and look for them?"

"They're gone. I'd wager..." The instant the words were out, he stilled. Rushing to the wardrobe, he tossed items to the floor, searching for the leather pouch. Beginning to panic, he pushed aside his long duster, letting out a relieved breath.

Lifting it, his blood began to boil. The pouch should be thicker, heavier. Standing, he dumped the money onto the bed and began counting. Jaw clenched tight, he finished, turning to Ma.

"Half the money is gone."

Ma sat down on the edge of the bed. "If it's gone, then so are Junior and Sissy."

"We have to find them." He stalked to the wardrobe, pulling out the old clothes he'd tucked away when they'd first arrived in Splendor. Ma gripped his arm, stopping his actions.

"They're long gone, Pa. We knew this day would come sometime. It's come about sooner than we'd thought."

"Junior stole from us. I can't let that go."

"Yes, you can. Half that money was going to Junior and Sissy anyway. You said so yourself. 'Sides, I think the girl is pregnant."

Pa dropped the dirt-encrusted clothes on the floor, gaze boring into hers. "Pregnant? By who?"

"Who do you think? Junior's been poking her for a long time. This was bound to happen. I sure don't want some crying brat around. It's better this way, Pa."

Throwing back his head, he stared at the ceiling, letting out a string of curses. "I've got plans for tomorrow, and they include Junior."

Ma already knew his intent, even though he'd never discussed it with her. "I'll take his place."

He glared at her, shaking his head. "No way in hell."

"I can shoot and ride as well as Junior."

Pa studied her, remembering their history. She was right. Until the last few years, she'd been involved in most robberies. No reason she couldn't partner with him tomorrow.

"Are you sure you want to do this, Ma? I can do it by myself. Or we can leave town with what's left of the money, go after a stage or two along the way to California."

"Tomorrow is the perfect time, while everyone is at the Pelletier ranch. I doubt the sheriff will leave more than two or three deputies in town. We'll never get a better chance."

Pacing the room, he stroked his jaw, his agitation returning. "If that boy had stayed just two more days. If he'd told me he wanted to leave."

"What would you have done? You would never have let him and Sissy leave. That's why they snuck out. They're probably halfway to California by now."

"Not with her pregnant." Pa scrubbed a hand over his face, a feral growl escaping. "Damn. This changes all my plans. A few more banks and we would've been able to quit, get a place like you've always wanted, where it's warm most of the year."

Lips parting, she walked toward him, placing a hand on his arm. "You remembered."

He snorted, mouth twisting into a sardonic grin. "You've put up with this life long enough, Ma. You deserve more than I've ever given you."

Swallowing, she pinched her eyes shut to stop tears from falling. "I would've done anything to be with you, Pa. Your life is my life. It always has been."

"Papa, you have to tie a ribbon at the end." Lucy stood at the mirror in her bedroom, studying the braid.

Chuckling, Hex removed the lid from her ribbon box. "What color?"

"Red."

He'd known the answer before asking. Securing the ribbon to her braid, he pulled out his pocket watch, checking the time.

"Chrissy and Cici will be here soon. Are you ready, Luce?"

Smiling, she shot him a quick nod before running to the front window. "How much longer until they get here, Papa?"

"Not long, Luce."

"There they are!" She ran to the front door, waiting with a five-year-old's impatience. The instant she heard the knock, Lucy pulled the door open. "Can we go now, Papa?"

"Luce. Use your manners."

Face falling, she grew quiet for a long moment before opening the door wide. "Would you like to come in?"

Christina hid her smile as she looked past Lucy to Hex. "Good morning."

Instead of responding, he walked to her, bending to kiss her cheek. "You look beautiful, Chrissy."

Glancing down at her brown coat, plain cotton dress, and sensible shoes, she didn't feel beautiful. "Well...thank you."

Hex glanced down to see her fingers clenched around the handles of a large fabric bag laden with supplies. "I'll take that."

Cocking her head to the side, her brows furrowed. "Are you going with us?"

"I'll accompany the three of you, stay for a while if you and the ladies need my help."

"That's wonderful of you." She held up the bag, handing it to him.

The church women were meeting at the church's community center to bake and prepare other food for the ranch rodeo tomorrow. The kitchen in back was equipped with three wood burning stoves, long counters, two sinks, and lengths of cabinets. The perfect place for a group of people to prepare large meals for weddings, birthdays, and community celebrations.

Hex and Christina walked several feet behind the girls, who skipped, laughed, and talked. The two got along better than sisters.

"Isabella told me two of Noah's horses were stolen last night and the thieves got away."

Reaching out, Hex threaded his fingers with Christina's, relieved when she didn't pull away. "What you may not know is the thieves left money for the horses and tack. Noah decided to let them go, figuring they must've had a reason for what they did."

She wasn't too surprised. Everyone who'd been in Splendor long knew of Noah's forgiving nature. "Do you know who they are?"

Hex thought of the young man and woman he'd seen most mornings walking the boardwalk, her arm through his. They were part of the four diners at the boardinghouse who'd witnessed the killing of the U.S. Marshal.

"Not yet. Dutch and Beau followed, but lost the trail. Dutch said it was two men." Hex wasn't as sure. Turning toward the center, he slowed their pace when he spotted the older man and woman who'd been at the table that night.

"Lucy and Cici. Wait a moment." He turned to Christina. "Will you stay with the girls while I speak with that couple?"

Following his gaze, she nodded. "They were there that night when the U.S. Marshal was murdered."

Rushing to catch up with them, he called after them until they stopped. Hex touched the brim of his hat, nodding at both.

"Good morning." He couldn't recall their last names, but remembered the older man was the uncle of the girl, and the older woman the aunt of the young man. At least, that's what they'd told Gabe the night of the shooting.

"Deputy."

"I wondered if you might know where I'd find the young man and woman who were at the table with you the night of the shooting."

Pa Groom gave Ma a worried look before his features hardened. "What would be your interest in them?"

"Nothing important. I wanted to follow up on a conversation the young man and I had last week. Are they at breakfast?"

Clearing his throat, Pa shook his head. "I haven't seen them this morning. Perhaps they're at the boardinghouse. They have been spending quite a bit of time together."

"Thank you. Enjoy your walk."

"Deputy." Pa and Ma watched him head back in the direction he'd come, seeing him join a woman and two young girls. The same people who'd shared a table not far from theirs that night.

"What do you think he wants, Pa?"

"I don't know, but it can't be good for us." Pa continued to watch the four until they disappeared into the building behind the church. "It will take him a while to discover Junior and Sissy are gone. By then, we'll have finished our business and be long gone."

Hex stayed for close to an hour, mainly to spend time with Christina. The women had little need of his help. Even so, he brought in wood for the stoves, relocated tables, and helped carry supplies into the center. All the while, he never lost sight of Christina.

He watched her interact with the women, talking and laughing as if she'd been living in Splendor for years. Everyone liked her. Men and women. Today, they gravitated toward her, wanting to work side-by-side as they made pies, breads, and casseroles for the rodeo.

In addition to the baking, she kept watch on Cici and Lucy, who played with other girls at the other end of the center. Warmth spread through him. She was everything he ever wanted in a woman. And she loved Lucy.

"Thought you might be here." Turning away from Christina, he saw Zeke approach.

"What brings you in here?" Hex thought it might be because of a certain female attorney rolling out dough next to Christina.

"No reason." But Zeke's gaze moved past him to where Francesca worked.

A corner of Hex's mouth lifted. "You sure?"

Resting his hands on his hips, Zeke shook his head. "She won't talk to me, other than being pleasant. If we pass on the boardwalk, she'll nod or say hello without stopping." He chanced a look at Francesca.

"Why's that?"

Pinching the bridge of his nose, Zeke's jaw clenched. "She saw me having supper with another woman at the Eagle's Nest. Frannie arrived with a couple of the women who'd come west with her. The look on her face..." He shook his head.

Hex's brows drew together. "Were you courting Frannie?"

He winced. "I might've mentioned not being interested in any woman except her."

"So who is this other woman, and why did you take her to supper if you had an interest in Frannie?"

"I'm not telling you her name, but she's a widow who arrived in town a few months ago with her son. She's real shy, spends her time taking care of the boy and doing some seamstress work for Allie Coulter." The moment the words were out, he knew he'd said too much.

"Real pretty, not tall, brown hair, and green eyes?"

Zeke groaned. "Yeah. I don't know why I invited her to supper."

"Maybe you weren't ready to make a commitment to Frannie. Could've been spending time with another woman was your way of figuring out your feelings for her."

"If so, it was one of the stupidest decisions I ever made. The widow is now being courted by a local rancher, and the woman I want won't speak to me."

Clasping his brother on the back, Hex grinned. "If you're serious about her, give it time. Keep inviting her out, walk her home after work, let her see she's the one you want."

Zeke chuckled without a hint of humor. "She's a stubborn woman with a great deal of pride. It could take years to get her to change her mind."

Hex glanced at the two women who'd secured the attention of the Boudreaux brothers. Both beautiful, smart, kind. He then thought of Alana Hanrahan, and how his short acquaintance with her could've ruined what was building between him and Christina.

He may not have any idea how to help Zeke, but felt for his brother. "I believe it will work out between the two of you."

"Thanks, Hex. Whether there's still hope for a future with Frannie or not, I've learned a real important lesson, one you might consider."

"What's that?"

"When you find the right woman, don't let her slip through your fingers."

Chapter Twenty-Six

Sunday brought a clear sky and little wind. The perfect day for the rodeo and shooting competition. Wagons filled with food began leaving town right after breakfast. The women drove while men rode alongside, saddlebags packed with ammunition. Most carried rifles, with six-shooters strapped around their waists.

Gabe accompanied his wife, Lena, and their children, Jackson and baby Emma. Behind them, they could hear a group of his deputies talking and laughing, ready to display their skills.

At points where the trail narrowed, several wagons would slow, waiting for those ahead of them to proceed. There were times it seemed the entire town was deserting Splendor.

Hex and Zeke rode horses alongside Christina, Cici, and Lucy in a wagon. The girls held pies in their laps, while breads, casseroles, and other food had been carefully packed in the back.

An air of excitement filled the air, the townsfolk and neighboring ranchers ready for a day of celebration. Christmas, Independence Day, spring dance, and fall festival brought everyone together. After today, the ranch rodeo might be added to the list of annual festivals.

Redemption's Edge buzzed with activity when Hex and his group rode up. Empty wagons were already parked in a large field. Well over a hundred people wandered around, some arranged tables for food, others set up the shooting competition, while a good number of the men discussed rodeo events.

The rodeo would happen first, followed by the shooting competition. Food and drinks would be sold all day. A large corral had been established for children with several swings, wooden throwing rings and wands for *Game of Graces*, and bats, balls, and gloves for baseball.

Hex and Zeke helped Christina and the girls to the ground, then carried the food to tables already filling with food. The girls didn't wait before running to join the other children playing in the corral, Christina watching until Ginny Pelletier waved at her. It was then she felt a hand resting on her lower back, knowing it was Hex.

"We need to talk to Dax and Luke about the rodeo and competition." Hex stood next to her. A few feet away, Zeke talked with Bull Mason and Dirk Masters, the two Pelletier foremen.

"Are you competing in any of the rodeo events?"

A self-deprecating chuckle left his lips. "Zeke plans to enter a couple events. I've volunteered to help with livestock, tack, and whatever else they need done. I'll join the shooting competition with four other deputies."

"I'll be sure to watch. I should go join the other women. We're hoping to make a good deal of money for the school and church."

Uncaring who watched, Hex touched his mouth to her cheek, wanting to do more. "Come watch some of the rodeo when you have a chance."

"I plan to." Grinning, she turned away, waving to Francesca as she approached the tables.

The butterflies in her stomach came alive whenever Hex was near, exploding when he kissed her, settled a hand on her back, or took her hand in his. His attention spoke of a deeper interest than friends. He asked to court her, which she'd readily accepted.

Since then, their relationship had become less strained, his touches more frequent. His attention excited her, made her desire expand.

He'd kissed her more than once, each time the heat blossoming through her in waves of pleasure. She wanted him to do more, although she didn't quite know what.

"Good morning, Frannie."

"Hello, Chrissy. Wonderful day for a festival."

"Yes, it is." She looked around, amazed at the amount of food already set out, and people were still arriving. "I don't know what we're going to do with all of this."

Frannie took a bite of a sweet bread slice she'd already purchased. "Believe me." She nodded behind her. "Those men out there are going to work up their appetites with all the activity. I doubt there'll be anything left by the end of the day."

"Judging by what Hex and Zeke eat each night, you're probably right."

Frannie looked away, absently readjusting the food on the table. Christina had seen her do the same the day before when Zeke had entered the community center. Fussing, taking furtive glances at him, which wasn't at all like the efficient attorney she knew.

"What's going on between you and Zeke?"

Glancing up, Francesca's shocked expression almost made Christina chuckle. "I don't know what you mean."

"I know it isn't my business, but you haven't accepted a single invitation to share supper with us in weeks. I thought you and Zeke were doing so well."

Letting out a ragged sigh, Frannie gave a slow shake of her head. "So did I."

"What happened?"

She shrugged, clasping her hands together as she smiled at the other women. "I don't know. It seems he's developed an interest in another woman." Clearing her throat, her voice lowered to a whisper. "Two friends and I went to the Eagle's Nest for supper one night, and Zeke was there with another woman. She was, well...quite lovely. It was obvious he had an interest in her."

Zeke hadn't mentioned Francesca in a couple weeks. Christina now knew why. "What did you do?"

She shrugged, face clouding. "Nothing. I had supper with my friends while he placed all his attention on the other woman. We left, and I haven't spoken with him since."

Christina had never known Zeke to be dishonest about anything. She was certain his attraction to Francisca had been intense, serious. His mood had been off for a while. Instead of the usual positive and talkative deputy, he'd been morose, quiet. Both quite unlike him.

"He hasn't tried to talk to you since that night?"

Frannie swallowed, not meeting her gaze. "Zeke did come by my office a few times, but I sent him off." She glanced across the open expanse to where the men were preparing for the rodeo, her gaze locking on Zeke. "I didn't want to hear excuses, and I certainly had no desire to learn about the woman who'd drawn his attention away from me. We've seen each other around town several times, but there isn't much to say."

Christina's expression softened even more. "Of course there's a lot to say. Maybe it wasn't what you thought."

Francesca caught her bottom lip between her teeth, saying nothing for several long moments. "I know. It's just..." Her gaze again focused on Zeke. "He stopped coming by my office. I believe he's put it behind him and moved on."

She didn't talk of her past, the way her fiancé back east had done the same. Francesca had been to supper with her parents when she spotted the man she'd loved for years with another woman.

In that instance, her father had confronted him, taken her fiancé by the lapels and shoved him against a wall. He'd stood over him, warning the man to never come to their house again and never contact her, ending what she'd thought was a relationship built on love and mutual respect. It had been a painful lesson, realizing neither had been true. The only person she'd shared the story with was Rachel Pelletier, the friend who'd invited her to travel to Splendor.

"He hasn't put it behind him, Frannie. I'm certain of it. Today might be the perfect time to speak with him." She followed her friend's gaze, watching Zeke laugh with the other men.

"He doesn't appear to be suffering any negative effects of us not seeing each other anymore." Then Zeke looked her way and Frannie stilled. Their gazes locked, neither breaking the contact until one of the men clasped Zeke on the shoulder, breaking the spell.

Tired of discussing her problems, Francesca forced a smile. "How are you and Hex doing?"

A wistful expression washed over Christina's face. "Everything is wonderful," she breathed out. "Did I tell you he asked to court me?"

Francesca's brows shot upward. "No. When did this happen?"

"Not long ago. He's been so sweet and attentive. I already know how I feel."

"Hex just needs to come to terms with what he wants," Francesca added.

Christina let her attention wander to where he stood near the barn. Taking a step forward, she narrowed her gaze on the voluptuous woman in front of him. *Alana.*

A moment later, Hex reached out, putting his hand on her arm. At first, Christina thought it was from affection. Instead, he dropped his hold on her, his features contorted as he shook his head, saying something to her before walking away.

"Who is that woman?" Francesca asked.

Christina let out an anxious breath. "Alana Hanrahan. Her family arrived in town weeks ago. She's been trying to attract Hex ever since."

"It doesn't appear he has any interest in her, Chrissy. Wait. Is she part of the family who opened the new saloon?"

"That's her. She really is beautiful. I doubt many men turn her down."

At that moment, Hex walked toward them, his features inscrutable. Christina's heart pounded the closer he got. She stiffened, expecting bad news. Instead, he stopped in front of her, gripped her shoulders, and covered her mouth with his.

"Are you ready, Ma?" He wore his worn trail clothes instead of the suit the town had become used to seeing him in.

His wife hadn't changed from her normal clothes. There was no need, as she'd be the lookout, making sure no one became suspicious while he did his work inside the bank. He'd heard Horace Clausen kept everything locked up tight in the vault. One that would require dynamite to open. But he also learned Clausen kept a decent amount of money in a smaller safe in his office. Not a lot, but enough to fund them on their way to California.

"Ready as I'll ever be, Pa."

He'd purchased horses and tack earlier in the week from Noah, keeping them in the livery until early this morning. He'd made arrangements to retrieve them while the rest of the town headed to the Pelletier ranch. Noah figured they were just two more people headed toward the festivities away from town.

Noah told him two deputies had stayed to protect the town. Beau Davis and Cash Coulter. Pa knew them to be experienced and skilled. They'd been deputies for years, coming to Splendor not long after the War Between the States ended.

"It's time." Pa made another check of the room, satisfied they'd left nothing behind.

They used the back stairs, seeing no one before stepping outside. The horses waited for them, Pa's saddlebags were empty, ready for their take from the bank. Ma's held personal belongings. Each held a rifle in their scabbard.

Looking around, seeing no one watching, Pa nodded at her to mount up. When she was settled into the saddle, he followed, checking the six-shooters around his waist.

She rode around the hotel first, stopping when she reached the main street. The bank stood on the opposite side, a few buildings down. The boardwalk was almost deserted. Mostly older men and women. No one who'd stop them from their plans.

The deputies were nowhere in sight. Ma shifted in the saddle, motioning Pa forward. Guiding his horse across the street, he rode to behind the bank. The buildings across from them were empty houses owned by Noah and his wife. It was the best opportunity they'd have to leave town with a large haul.

Perhaps their largest ever.

Chapter Twenty-Seven

Jerome rolled the cylinders of both revolvers, noting all carried a bullet. Theo and Byron did the same, each giving a terse nod at their older brother.

They'd broken camp before sunup, hitting the trail to Splendor with one intent—to get their money from Groom and leave the territory.

Three hours later, Jerome had pulled off the trail before arriving at one end of town, watching as wagon after wagon drove north to Redemption's Edge. Waiting, they found positions not far from the St. James Hotel. It was as he'd suspected. The town appeared to be almost deserted.

Jerome motioned for Theo to ride the streets, searching for deputies. It didn't take long before he returned. He'd spotted two deputies, men he hadn't seen before.

"I told them I was passing through, hoped to get a couple drinks and fill my stomach. They directed me to the boardinghouse or McCall's." Theo snorted, relaxing his grip on the reins. "One of them told me about the goings on at the Pelletier ranch, suggested I ride out before leaving town."

"Where did you find them?" Jerome asked.

"One was sitting outside the jail, the other near Chinatown."

"Look." Byron pointed toward the hotel. "Isn't that Groom?"

A feral grin twisted Jerome's mouth. "It is."

"There's a woman on the other side of the street," Byron added. "Is she Groom's wife?"

Jerome moved his horse forward a few yards, his eyes narrowing on the woman. "I never saw her, but she's watching him ride behind the bank. Damn. The old man's going to rob the bank."

"What do you want to do?" Theo asked.

Jerome sat back in his saddle, watching Groom while considering their next move. He'd expected to surprise the man in his room, tie him up, take what was theirs, and leave. What he and his brothers were watching meant a different plan, one requiring patience. One which would garner them much more than what Groom owed them.

"We wait until he's finished and leaves the bank. If he doesn't attract the attention of the deputies, then we follow them out of town."

Byron leaned over his saddlehorn, sneering. "And let him know what happens to people who try to cross us."

Pa flattened himself against the outside wall, took a minute to look around before creeping to the back door of the bank. It took less than a minute to disable the feeble lock and step inside.

He wasted no time getting to the front of the bank and Clausen's office. In the corner, a small safe had been located beside a tall file cabinet. Checking the windows, he relaxed. The ones located on the side walls had been located too high for anyone to look inside.

Those facing the street were made of opaque glass. He'd heard Clausen had made the change from clear glass after a robbery a few years before, the same time he'd purchased a more secure safe in a room with a barred entrance. Groom didn't care about the large safe holding most of the bank's money. Whatever he found in the smaller one would be enough. It was time for him to get to work.

Dropping to his knees beside the safe, he felt almost giddy with excitement. It was an older model, at least thirty years, with few improvements of new safes. And easier to break into.

He studied the front and one side wall. Reaching around the metal box, he tried to move it away toward the center of the room, but the weight was more than he could handle.

He retrieved a small, leather case. To most, it appeared to be a wallet secured with leather strips.

Laying it down, he unfolded it, revealing tools he knew well.

As a younger man, Groom had held an apprentice position with a safe manufacturing company in New York. He'd stayed almost ten years before deciding the job would never make him rich. After resigning, he'd put the skills he learned to good use.

Banks in small towns weren't prepared for what he could do. Eventually, the spread of railroads carrying money and gold in safes proved a huge boon to his finances. He'd joined a gang of men who didn't care what it took to relieve others of their wealth. They'd welcomed his skills, until the leaders had been shot by Pinkerton agents during one risky job.

Groom had escaped. Those not killed scattered, heading in all directions. He'd heard many were tracked down, stood trial, and were escorted to prison in shackles...or hung. Yes, he'd been fortunate.

Studying the safe, he picked up a tool and went to work.

Redemption's Edge

"Zeke is getting ready to ride. Let's go watch him." Christina tugged on the fabric of Francesca's sleeve, who tugged right back.

Although she turned toward the corral where Zeke climbed over the fence, walking toward the unbroken horse, she dug in her heels. "I should stay here. Help the other women."

"You should take some time to watch the rodeo. Have you ever seen one before?"

"Has *anyone* here seen a rodeo?" Francesca countered.

"Someone had to or they wouldn't have suggested it." Christina continued to tug on her arm. "Just a few minutes, Frannie. It will be fun."

Groaning, she lifted her head to see Zeke readying to mount, two men holding the horse still. Her gaze was riveted on him, feet moving without thought toward the arena. She began to walk faster, Christina right behind her.

Francesca's pace slowed, heart beating a frantic pace when he took the reins and swung into the saddle. The horse stilled for one...two...three seconds before exploding into the air.

She gasped, hands rising to her throat. The horse continued bucking, Zeke holding on with both hands, his features severe in concentration. Francesca had never seen him so focused and determined.

The group of men around the corral roared when the horse jumped several feet into the air and twisted. Zeke flew into the air, arms flailing as he fell to the ground, landing on his back.

The crowd hushed, women gasping when he didn't move. Francesca moved toward the gate, ready to run to him, then stopped. She looked around for the pretty woman he'd escorted to supper. Perhaps she was the one he'd want to see.

Watching from the corral, she waited until he sat up, fighting for breath. Satisfied he hadn't killed himself, Francesca headed back to the tables. She didn't want to be too close if the woman he'd been seeing showed up.

"Zeke did great. Don't you think?" Christina caught up with her, falling into step. "Bull said he's in the top five. They're going to go another round."

Whirling around, Francesca fisted both hands on her hips. "Another round? He could get killed, or break an arm, a leg, or his back. I've never seen anything so ridiculous."

Christina bit her lower lip, holding back a grin. "I thought you no longer cared what happened to Zeke."

Francesca huffed out a frustrated breath. "I don't. But I hate to see anyone get hurt, even a miscreant such as Zeke." Reaching their table, she picked up a slice of sweet bread, taking a large bite.

"If you don't need me for a few minutes, I'm going to see how the girls are doing, and watch the roping contest." In truth, Christina wanted to see Hex. He wasn't competing in the rodeo events, which might give them time to visit.

She touched her lips, still feeling their kiss. It had been intense, longer than others, and unexpected. Most astounding, he'd kissed her in front of a good number of people, as if he'd claimed her and wanted everyone to know it.

"There's more than enough help here, Chrissy. Go find your man."

She opened her mouth to protest, then closed it. If the kiss was what she thought, he was very much *her man.*

Splendor

Groom emerged from the bank, careful to search for anyone watching before closing the door. According to the clock hanging in the office, it had taken him less than ten minutes from the time he entered until leaving. A few hundred dollars were stuffed into a pouch taken from Clausen's desk, and now hidden in the waistband of his pants.

Reaching his horse, he again glanced around. This time, he stilled. One of the deputies was at the far end of the street, near Chinatown, talking to one of the men rebuilding from the fire.

Taking advantage of the deputy's temporary diversion, he swung into the saddle. Leaning low over the horse's neck, he urged the animal toward Ma.

Meeting her in front of Allie Coulter's dress shop, he nodded away from the jail and Chinatown, toward the church.

They rode slowly, not wanting to garner attention from anyone who might be watching. Passing the community center, the two picked up their pace.

They rode for about a mile before Pa urged his horse forward, picking up speed. Ma followed, both beginning to relax. They'd already planned their escape route. South, then west, then south again to Salt Lake City. From there, they'd take the train to San Francisco, where the opportunities were wide and deep.

A smile crept across Pa's face. They'd done it. The amount wasn't as large as hoped, but it was more than enough to get them to California. He'd buy her a house, one where Ma could plant a garden, meet the neighbors, and begin a normal life.

Feeling the future open before them, Pa never heard the pounding of horse hooves behind them. Didn't glance behind them to see three riders, all with their guns drawn. Never felt the bullet pierce his heart, or hear Ma's scream when a second bullet tore through her neck.

And neither felt their bodies slam to the ground because they were already dead.

Chapter Twenty-Eight

Redemption's Edge

The five-man team of deputies lined up for the rifle contest. Hex, Zeke, Shane, Hawke, and Beth Evans prepared their ammunition and checked the breeze. It had been unusually still, the wind almost nonexistent. The perfect day for their competition.

"You ready, Shane?" Dirk Masters stood a few feet away. He managed the competitors while Bull Mason handled the targets.

For the rifle competition, tin cans were placed on stands set at fifty yards away. The second round would be at seventy-five, the third at one hundred.

Since they were shooting as teams, there'd be no individual winners, which would allow Noah to be part of a team. As a Union Army sharpshooter, he'd been known to make kill shots beyond the capability of other men. Instead of joining, he preferred to watch with his wife by his side.

Bull was the other expert shooter, but he'd also declined to participate, deciding to work with the targets.

"I'm ready." Stepping to the line Dirk had drawn, he sighted the rifle, squeezing off a shot. The can flew up and backward.

The other four deputies hit their marks, prompting Bull to place cans at seventy-five yards. Again, all five deputies blew their targets off the stand. The same happened at one hundred yards, making them the team to beat.

Smiles on their faces, the five left to watch the other teams. After less than an hour, two teams had tied for first—the deputies and Pelletier ranch hands.

Flipping a coin, Dirk announced the Redemption's Edge men would go first. This time, Bull set the distances at sixty, eighty, and one-hundred-ten yards. They lined up, Travis Dixon shooting first, hitting his target. The next three men did the same before Wyatt Jackson prepared to shoot.

Before lifting his rifle, he turned at a loud shout. Beau Davis jumped from his horse before coming to a stop, hurrying toward Gabe.

"We've got trouble in town. Horace Clausen made his usual Sunday afternoon visit to the bank. The door of the small safe he keeps in his office stood open. A few hundred dollars is missing."

"Did you or Cash see anything?"

"Sorry, Gabe. Whoever did this got in and out without us noticing. A woman from the St. James saw a man and woman ride out of town, but she didn't recognize them."

"Did she see which direction they went?"

"South."

By now, all his deputies stood around, as did many others. He found Dax in the crowd. "Sorry to cut this short, but we need to get back to town."

"Do you need help?"

"Thanks, but we'll take care of it. You enjoy the rest of the celebration. We had a grand time. Will you make sure our women and children get back to town safely?"

"You know we will."

"Thanks." Gabe clasped Dax on the shoulder, motioning for his deputies to follow him to their horses.

Byron threw the last handful of dirt on the bodies, standing aside to let Theo and Jerome sweep brush over the shallow graves. Afterward, they covered the ground with shrub. Located a dozen yards off the trail, they doubted anyone would ever find them.

Brushing dirt down his pants, Byron turned to his brothers. "Money's stashed away, Jerome. We should get out of here."

Jerome stared at the spot where they'd buried the Grooms, feeling no remorse. He'd given them plenty of time to settle their debt. Instead, they chosen to rob the bank and ride out. It had been a fatal decision.

For the Taggert men, the money taken from the saddlebags guaranteed a new start. They had enough to buy land and start the ranch they'd talked about for years. Maybe marry and have children. For the first time since taking off on their own, Jerome saw a good future.

"You're right. Which way do you boys want to go?"

Theo's mouth twisted into a grin. "I've heard there's real good land in Utah."

Byron leaned on his saddlehorn, glancing between his brothers. "You'll get no objection from me."

Pressing his hat farther down on his head, Jerome gave a brisk nod. "Then Utah it is."

Splendor

The search lasted two days, Gabe and the men who'd ridden with him returning without the robbers or money. Telegrams had already been sent to lawmen within a five hundred mile radius about the couple. Gabe believed it would be a miracle if they were ever caught.

After the woman from the hotel gave a detailed description of the people she saw, it hadn't taken long to establish their true identity. Pa and Ma Groom had been in town all along. Even with Gabe assuring him he wasn't at fault, Hawke cursed himself for not heeding Hex's advice to bring them to the jail for more questions.

"What about the three men who shot the U.S. Marshal in the boardinghouse?" Caleb leaned against the desk at the jail.

Cash scrubbed a hand down his face. "In my opinion, they're long gone. Hex, Zeke, and Hawke almost got to them, but they split up. I'm almost certain they're the ones who shot Luke. Afterward, they took off. I don't understand why they stayed around after killing Marshal Mulvaney."

Dutch leaned back in his chair, features drawn. "I doubt we'll ever know."

Hex stalked toward Christina's house, exhausted from almost three days with little sleep. He and the other deputies had returned a few hours earlier, met for beers at the Dixie, then dispersed, some going to the jail, others going home. He'd made a quick stop at his house to clean up and change clothes before heading out, hoping she'd saved some supper for him.

Lifting his hand, he rapped on her door. It opened almost immediately.

"Hex." She reached out, taking his hand to draw him inside. Closing the door, she studied him, seeing the fatigue on his face. "Have you eaten?"

"Not for hours."

"Sit down. I'll prepare a plate for you." Before she could turn away, he wrapped an arm around her waist, dragging her to him.

Cupping her face in his hands, Hex covered her mouth with his. Hearing her soulful moan, he deepened the kiss, his hands moving to her back, pressing her against him. Moving his lips along her jaw, down the soft column of her neck, he felt her squirm against him. Pleasure blazed through his body. Wanting more, he tightened his hold, capturing her mouth again.

"Hex." Christina's breathless groan pierced through his haze of desire.

"We have to stop, sweetheart."

"What?" Her eyes were glassy, confused.

His hold relaxed, but he didn't let go. Resting his forehead against hers, Hex closed his eyes.

"Are the girls asleep?"

Brows furrowing, she nodded. "For at least an hour."

Sucking in a breath, he took both her hands, guiding her to the sofa. "We should talk."

Christina's heart sank at the resigned tone in his voice. She did as he'd asked, trying to create distance between them, but he wouldn't loosen his grip on her hands.

Hex stared down at their joined hands, rubbing his thumbs over the back of hers. His jaw clenched, throat worked as he considered his next words. With slow purpose, he lifted his gaze to hers, seeing the confusion in her eyes, lines of worry around her mouth.

"I suppose I fell in love with you on the trail from Big Pine." He continued to softly move his thumbs over her hands.

Christian gasped, her heartbeat accelerating.

"I've been a fool, taking so long to let you know, Chrissy. More so when I hurt you by being seen with Alana. Which you already know meant nothing." Clearing his throat, he shifted on the sofa. "I don't know if you could ever love me, but—"

"I could," she interrupted. "I mean, I *do* love you, Hex."

A slow smile curved his lips at the rose tint spreading over her cheeks. "That's real good, Chrissy. If you're sure…"

"I'm very sure, Hex."

Sliding to the floor in front of her, his gaze met hers. "You're the best woman I've ever known. Fact is, you're everything to me, Chrissy. Would you consider marrying me…be my wife?"

She ignored the tears forming, throwing her arms around him. "Yes, Hex! I would be honored to be your wife."

Epilogue

One month later...

Hex kissed his wife, taking Christina's hand in his to walk past their friends for the first time as Mr. and Mrs. Hezekiah Boudreaux. Zeke held hands with Lucy and Cici, both skipping along with huge smiles on their faces.

Every few steps, one of Hex's friends slapped him on the back as they passed by, the women murmuring congratulations to Christina. Approaching the entrance to the church, Hex turned them around.

"I hope you'll all join us at the community center. I do believe the women have set up quite the spread."

Cheers and applause followed his announcement. It took little time to gather behind the church. Sure enough, the women had outdone themselves. The tables groaned with the amount of food. Fried chicken, sliced ham, roast beef, beans, potatoes, sweet potato pie, stewed fruits, puddings, and a variety of cakes.

Hex and Christina welcomed their friends as they arrived. While most of their guests went straight for the food, several stood in groups around the large room.

Once the last person had given their congratulations, Francesca joined them. "It's time for the band to start."

Hex glanced between her and his wife. "All right."

Both women chuckled at his befuddled expression. "It means you and Chrissy start it off with a dance."

His brows shot up. "We do?"

Francesca bit her lower lip. "It's always that way, Hex. Don't worry, after a minute or so, others will join you."

He glanced at Christina, wincing. "If it's expected."

Smiling, she took his hand, leading him to the open space reserved for dancing. Facing her, Hex took her in his arms as the band began to play.

"They are so perfect for each other." Francesca glanced at her friend, Georgina, the newest nurse at the clinic, and Rachel Pelletier. "For a while, I thought Hex would never see what was right in front of him."

She thought of Zeke. Another example of a man unable or unwilling to open his eyes to what could be. They hadn't known each other long, but in that time, her heart had softened for the charming deputy. Francesca still didn't understand what she'd done to change his mind.

Rachel watched the new couple dance. "It takes some men longer than others. Most don't take much time thinking about love, marriage, and a future."

Georgina nodded, but her attention focused on a man across the room. Dutch McFarlin spoke with a group of deputies, laughing before pulling a flask from his pocket and passing it around.

She hadn't spoken with him since those few minutes at the clinic when Luke had been shot. This was one of those times when she wished for courage. If she were strong, like the two women beside her, she'd try to get his attention instead of standing here hoping.

"Good afternoon, Miss Wise."

She jerked her head up to see Dutch standing next to her. Georgina clasped her hands so he wouldn't see them shake.

"Hello, Deputy McFarlin."

"Dutch."

She felt her face flush. "Yes, Dutch. But you must call me Georgina."

His grin was fast and sincere. He held out his hand. "Would you honor me with a dance?"

Heart pounding, she licked her lips before placing her hand in his. "That would be lovely."

Francesca watched them join the others on the dance floor, a seed of envy growing. She knew it was ridiculous. Georgina deserved to have a man such as Dutch pay attention to her.

"Miss O'Reilly?"

Startled, she turned to face a man she'd seen about town but never formally met. She wondered how he knew her name. "Yes."

"I'm one of Gabe's deputies. Shane Banderas. Would you dance with me?"

Features softening, she took the hand he offered. "I'd love to dance with you."

Zeke stood near the food tables, his jaw clenching when he spotted Shane escort Francesca to the dance area. Hex had told him more than once to talk with her, explain what she saw at the Eagle's Nest. Instead, his pride stopped him.

Zeke had a decision to make. From what he was watching, he'd better make it soon.

Thank you for taking the time to read Mystery Mesa. If you enjoyed it, please consider telling your friends or posting a short review. Word of mouth is an author's best friend and much appreciated.

Watch for book sixteen in the Redemption Mountain series, Thunder Valley.

If you want in on all the backstage action of my historical westerns, join my VIP Reader's Group: https://geni.us/PzgXR

Join my Newsletter to be notified of Pre-Orders and New Releases:
https://www.shirleendavies.com/

I care about quality, so if you find an error, please contact me via email at
shirleen@shirleendavies.com

About the Author

Shirleen Davies writes romance. She is the best-selling author of books in the romantic suspense, military romantic suspe3ns historical western romance, and contemporary western romance genres. Shirleen grew up in Southern California, attended Oregon State University, and has degrees from San Diego State University and the University of Maryland. Her passion is writing emotionally charged stories of flawed people who find redemption through love and acceptance. She lives with her husband in a beautiful town in northern Arizona.

I love to hear from my readers!

Send me an email: shirleen@shirleendavies.com
Visit my Website: www.shirleendavies.com
Sign up to be notified of New Releases:
www.shirleendavies.com
Check out all of my Books:
www.shirleendavies.com/books.html
Comment on my Blog:
www.shirleendavies.com/blog.html
Follow me on Amazon:
http://www.amazon.com/author/shirleendavies
Follow my on BookBub:
https://www.bookbub.com/authors/shirleen-davies

Other ways to connect with me:

Facebook Author Page:
http://www.facebook.com/shirleendaviesauthor
Twitter: www.twitter.com/shirleendavies
Pinterest: http://pinterest.com/shirleendavies
Instagram:
https://www.instagram.com/shirleendavies_author/

Books by Shirleen Davies

Historical Western Romance Series

MacLarens of Fire Mountain

Tougher than the Rest, Book One
Faster than the Rest, Book Two
Harder than the Rest, Book Three
Stronger than the Rest, Book Four
Deadlier than the Rest, Book Five
Wilder than the Rest, Book Six

Redemption Mountain

Redemption's Edge, Book One
Wildfire Creek, Book Two
Sunrise Ridge, Book Three
Dixie Moon, Book Four
Survivor Pass, Book Five
Promise Trail, Book Six
Deep River, Book Seven
Courage Canyon, Book Eight
Forsaken Falls, Book Nine
Solitude Gorge, Book Ten
Rogue Rapids, Book Eleven
Angel Peak, Book Twelve
Restless Wind, Book Thirteen
Storm Summit, Book Fourteen
Mystery Mesa, Book Fifteen
Thunder Valley, Book Sixteen, Coming Next in the Series!

MacLarens of Boundary Mountain

Colin's Quest, Book One,
Brodie's Gamble, Book Two
Quinn's Honor, Book Three
Sam's Legacy, Book Four
Heather's Choice, Book Five
Nate's Destiny, Book Six
Blaine's Wager, Book Seven
Fletcher's Pride, Book Eight
Bay's Desire, Book Nine
Cam's Hope, Book Ten

Romantic Suspense

Eternal Brethren, Military Romantic Suspense

Steadfast, Book One
Shattered, Book Two
Haunted, Book Three
Untamed, Book Four
Devoted, Book Five
Faithful, Book Six
Exposed, Book Seven,
Undaunted, Book Eight, Coming Next in the Series!

Peregrine Bay, Romantic Suspense

Reclaiming Love, Book One
Our Kind of Love, Book Two
Edge of Love, Coming Next in the Series!

Contemporary Romance Series

MacLarens of Fire Mountain

Second Summer, Book One
Hard Landing, Book Two
One More Day, Book Three
All Your Nights, Book Four
Always Love You, Book Five
Hearts Don't Lie, Book Six
No Getting Over You, Book Seven
'Til the Sun Comes Up, Book Eight
Foolish Heart, Book Nine

Burnt River

Thorn's Journey
Del's Choice
Boone's Surrender

The best way to stay in touch is to subscribe to my newsletter. Go to www.shirleendavies.com and subscribe in the box at the top of the right column that asks for your email. You'll be notified of new books before they are released, have chances to win great prizes, and receive other subscriber-only specials.

Avalanche Ranch Press, LLC
PO Box 12618
Prescott, AZ 86304

Mystery Mesa is a work of fiction. Names, characters, places, and incidents are either products of the author's imagination or used fictitiously. Any resemblance to actual events, locales, or persons, living or dead, is wholly coincidental.

Made in the USA
Monee, IL
26 May 2020